Bridging the Gap

Collection of short stories

Sarla Bhatia

S.K. Bhatia

New Delhi

First Edition : 2015

© Sarla Bhatia
S.K. Bhatia

Cover Illustration: Aloke Sinha

❑ Information contained in this book has been published by Virtuous Publications and has been obtained by its authors from sources believed to be reliable and are correct to the best of their knowledge. However, the publisher and its authors shall in no event be liable for any errors, omissions or damages arising out of use of this information and specifically disclaim any implied warranties or merchantability or fitness for any particulars use.

Mktg. & Sales : A-8, Hosiery Complex, Phase-II Extension
Noida 201305, U.P., INDIA
Telephone : 0120-4253470, 71, 77-80
Fax : 0120-4253478
Website : www.virtuouspublications.com
E-mail : contact@virtuouspublications com

Printed at: VPS Engineering Impex (Pvt) Ltd., Noida
Email : vps_8hc@yahoo.co.in

Preface

The authors in this book "Bridging the Gap" have written short stories on various interesting subjects. Every short story has a moralistic conclusion providing the readers with an insight and the joy of reading. Simple and expressive, one can easily relate to them (stories) and reflect. Life as we know is unknown and forever changing. The stories are about various aspects of life including individual struggles, social obligations, war and people, aims and aspirations, love and affection, lesson and experience and lot more. The content of the stories have been beautifully penned down, with in-depth details, that it takes the readers into an entirely different world. The authors have also given quite interesting characterizations, which though may appear like glimpses of our common day life or seem familiar, are yet loud with depth and meaning. The simple language and text makes them even more pleasurable to read.

Wonderfully written, we are sure our readers will thoroughly enjoy it.

– *Publisher*

Dedicated to Parents in Heaven

Sqn. Ldr. Chunni Lal Bhatia

Smt. Lilawati Bhatia

And

Shri Hira Nand Bhatia

Smt. Vidyawati Bhatia

Contents

The War of Yellow Brigades

IT is an amazing fable, from the diary of my ancestors. Two friends, Janos and Julius lived sixteen centuries ago, and met at the University of Takshila. Janos belonged to Kandhar in Afghanistan, and Julius was the prince of an area, consisting of present-day Kashmir. Julius would often go into a reverie. 'Our forests are dense and snow-clad mountains look sublime. Its valleys are rich in apples, pears, plums and apricots. And the fruit-gardens aside swirling rivulets provide heavenly living'. Janos would emphasise that, "Afghanistan is no less prosperous, where grapes, musk-melons, walnuts and almond trees grow in abundance. Trade and commerce in opium and carpets bring unmatched riches to my country". Alas! Their countrymen had lived as enemies for generations.

About 135 BC, five nomadic tribes known as the yueh-chih wrested, Central Asia and beyond, from the Greeks. These tribes united under the banner of Kushan, one of the five tribes. Their illustrious king, Kanishka'a (A.D. 78-144) empire stretched from Mathura in northern India to as far as the frontiers of China, Uzbekistan and Iran. A branch of the 'Silk Road' carrying luxury goods and arte-facts between Rome, India, and China passed through Afghanistan, where a transshipment centre existed at Balkh. Indian pilgrims travelling the Silk Road introduced

Buddhism to China where it flourished during the 2nd and 6th centuries. The world's largest Buddha statutes (53 metres high were installed about 4th and 5th centuries AD, the statues were destroyed in 2001. Trade and cultural achievement of the period were of world fame. Pieces of painted glass from Alexandria; plaster of Paris, bronzes, coppers, and Albatrosses from Rome, carved ivories from India, and lacquers from China were all over. A massive gold hoard of superb artistry existed at Sheberghan, west of Balkh. (Balkh and Bukhara are famous to this day).

After the death of Kanishka, hordes of tribes sprouted who boasted of amazingly accurate mounted archers, and their complete command of horsemanship, guerilla-like ferocious attacks, unpredictable maneuvers, and the speed of their strategic movements brought them overwhelming victories. Anarchy and splintered principalities came up all over those once prosperous lands. Peace and tranquility vanished from those territories. The boys were certain that they were descendants of the Kushan King Kanishka. They envied the 'Glory' of the past and rued the misery of their days!

At Takshila, the young men studied the best of the political and social philosophies of those days. Lord Buddha's dictum, "All woes are man made. The desire to conquer leads to 'Violence' which brings misery to mankind", planted the concept of non-violence in their minds. They also learnt Chanakya's strategy, that "If you cannot beat the enemy, then be friends with him". From the teaching of that 'political pundit', they also learnt that, 'Cooperation is profitable. Peaceful coexistence leads to economic prosperity and social & cultural developments. Wars leave behind dead bodies and ruins, alike, on the sides of the *victors and the vanquished*'.

However, after completing their studies when Julius and Janos reached their homes, they found the pots boiling in both kingdoms. Diplomatic exchanges were harsh and ominous. Julius's brother was to marry Rukhsana, the princess of Iran. The king of Persia wanted to give massive amounts of gold in dowry to Kashmir. How could the court at Kabul let this happen? It meant allowing carriage of riches through their lands to an enemy state, enabling it to buy armaments, and making it stronger. Janos used to meet Julius secretly to avoid the bloodshed which was imminent. He was aware that his country would be smashed to pieces if the armies of Iran and Kashmir jointly invaded Afghanistan.

Julius's father foresaw Kashmir's victory over Afghanistan and Julius's brother dreamed of owning the riches of Iran. The duo saw no reason for abandoning the marriage and dowry. They doubled up their preparations to crush their enemy. Julius and Janos continuously exchanged information regarding the war-preparations within their countries. In spite of deadly intentions of the opponents, the two angles of peace wanted to avoid confrontation at any cost!

Julius thought of a ploy. He said to his father, "Dad, let us change the colours of our army, from Red to Yellow. An astrologer tells me that yellow will bring us victory. It symbolizes the Sun the biggest source of energy in the Universe. The enemy will be confused on two counts; an unexpected look of our forces and the soldiers blending (colours) with the surrounding *marigold and 'sarson' (mustard) fields*" will evade their marksmen. The son is clever thought the King and ordered to bring about the change! Janos used the same, outwardly innocent, trick with the infuential people at the Afghan court. Thus, their Blue also became Yellow. By a coincidence the Iranian forces wore Yellow uniforms and displayed Sun on their flags. What a sight it would be, 'A spread of Yellow over miles and miles of the earth', thought Julius and Janos! But, would their ploy of one colour, Yellow lead to amity between the warring nations? God would be on their side, they hoped! They had one more trick up their sleeves, to outsmart the confronting forces.

Kashmiris marched ahead well before day-break. It was still dark. Thick and thundering clouds hung all over. A drizzle made the ground muddy and difficult to walk on. The war was on, anyway. Bugles and drums rented the air with their deafening noises. Horses could barely be kept in check. They stood on their hind legs when their riders pulled the reins too hard, awaiting the final orders to gallop ahead. Chaos was gradually changed into orderliness. The army of Kashmir marched past the Kyber-Pass, in formation and style. As the first contingent reached the outskirts of Kabul, its Commander got fluxed and confused. On the opposite side, the enemy's brigade, in Yellows, confronted them. He couldn't believe his eyes. Julius stood at the head of the forces at the opposite end!

"Had Julius already defeated Kabul?" "Had Afghanistan capitulated?" Or, "Had Julius joined the enemy?" Beguiled and bewildered, the Commander lost control of his men, who shouted, "We won! We won!" The news spread like wildfire to all nooks and corners of both the kingdoms. The men and women, from either domain embraced and hugged one another and went dancing and merry making. While the king of Kashmir and his son were engaged in resolving this enigma, they received another piece of disturbing news, "Iran and Afghanistan had committed to truce and peace". How did this happen?

Janos, on the advice of Julius, had amassed the Afghan soldiers at its western border with Iran. The Persians were only too pleased to see the enemy's soldiers clad in their Yellow colours. They believed it to be a sign of capitulation! Janos further announced, "Listen all men! My father offers a free passage to Rukhsana's dowry of gold and jewels, through its territory". The Persians were overjoyed and no longer felt like fighting the 'Olive-branch', so graciously displayed by the erstwhile enemy. There was fanfare all around.

Soldiers of the three armies having gone into ecstasy, the resolve to fight and kill waned, allbeit vanished. Julius rushed to his parental place to pacify and silence his father and brother. "Father, there are no longer Blues and Reds. My brother's marriage to the princess of Iran will usher in a new colour, Yellow, the symbol of the Sun, bestowing a bright future on one and all".

When the people of three kingdoms were merry making, gods too appeared in heavens above. The three pronged lightning strokes danced and pranced. Clouds thundered. Rains poured over the three kingdoms. Behold, some persons shouted! 'Luminous ball - shaped glows' stood on the lancers of soldiers. People believed that the Greek god Zesus and St. Erasmus were blessing them! Every one was sure that gods too wanted to celebrate through a Sound & Light Show.

My great grand father had written a note at the end of the above story, "The fable must be true. The ancient Greeks and Romans believed that the luminous glows were 'Corpo Santo-the body of a saint', and named them, "St Elmo's Fire', after their patron-saint Erasmus. Scientists proved, in the 18th century, that clouds carry electrified particles and form layers of high voltage of different strength. Lightning is caused by the flowing of currents between the electrically charged layers of clouds. The luminous-balls, “St Elmos’s Fire”, were nothing but static electric-charges on the sharp edges of soldiers’ lancers. The glows are visible when low clouds, lightning and rain occur about semi-dark environment, possibly when the armies faced each other.

Moreover, Blue, Yellow and Red are the three ‘prime colours’ of the White light’s spectrum. The Yellow colour lies at the middle of the Blue and the Red. It is a coincidence that the boys placed their faith on the Golden mean, to avoid a war. Remember my Children! Between the extremes, the magical solution lies midway”.

Be that as it may, let us rejoice that “Peace and Victory for All”, descended on those kingdoms without ‘Shooting an Arrow’! ❑❑

Julie, Oh Julie!

"What...at 11 O'clock...Punjabi Bagh", Shashi did not want to worry Ravi, her husband, at six in the morning, when the telephone bell rang. Ravi lay prostrate in his bed because of an accident, generally uable to sleep because of pain. Ravi, on learning of Didi's death, firstly sympathised and then advised "You must go to the cremation. It is a pity I am unable to join you. Don't worry, I can manage the two or three hours which you will be away. Sher Singh can take care of me in your absence. Serve me the pills before you depart".

I wondered if Madhav, our Driver, could ferry me to the Punjabi Bagh Crematorium. Still he was reassuring.

"Dont worry Madam, I have been that way once before. I will keep on the Ring Road...". "That is right" I intervened, "when we near the club in Punjabi Bagh, you can turn on the crossing towards Arya Samaj...". "Yes, yes, when we near that locality we can seek direction from the locals...".

Shashi dreads crowds. Delhi's traffic, on Ring Road in particular, is frightening. The three-wheelers and trucks numbers have grown unbelievably. To travel more than 20 km. from G.K.I to Punjabi Bagh is not easy any more. But then there is no choice to avoid such social obligations. Didi was so dear to her. How could she not be there at Didi's last rites... Shashi was awakened from her brooding.

"Madam, we have reached. I told you I know the way" said Madhav.

Shashi quietly alighted and walked towards the crematorium. There was no sign of any of the relatives. A little later she saw her Bhabi walk out of the office car, greeted her and asked "Have you rung up their house?" "Yes, they are about to leave. I reached here half an hour back. Samir had to examine one of his patients near here. And then his clinic opens at 10 o'clock. Though he will be slightly late but this was the best way to manage to reach here well in time".

Shashi and Bhabi, while waiting, exchanged some more tidings when the sharp noise of the tempo and cars caught their attention. "It looks like they have arrived". Bhabi nodded to agree, both of them walked towards the tempo. Didi's Arthi (dead body) was covered with shawls and flowers–marigolds, jasmines and roses. Those present could not hold back their tears. Tanvi was sobbing noisily. Babloo and Dabloo were crying hoarse. Shashi drew Tanvi aside, stroked her hair caressingly to say "Tanvi, you served your mother-in-law very patiently".

"Oh yes", Bhabi added "stop crying Tanvi. She suffered for long. For her it is her day of liberation from pain and misery".

"I visited her in Ganga Ram Hospital four months back. Her condition was pathetic. Didi could not recognise me. Even then she was past living..." said Shashi. But Tanvi replied "Auntie she recovered after that attack. Remember you visited us. Then she recognised you and hugged you".

"Oh yes, Tanvi, but that was Guddi's dedication for her mother. One month's uninterrupted nursing with the medicines that she brought from America. Parkinson's Disease is deadly in its advanced stage. Guddi performed a miracle".

Chanda, standing close to them, endorsed Shashi's sentiments, "Guddi proved that a daughter is a daughter always. She is a renowned doctor in one of the major hospitals. One full month Guddi was here to serve her mother".

Guddi is Didi's eldest child. Her correct name is Pratibha – the brilliant one. Shashi's thoughts at that time, in spite of the noises of priests chanting and wailing of the children, were seeking someone special.

"I dont see Julie here" she enquired in a low tone, to which Bhabhi's answer was "I wonder if the poor girl was informed at all".

Shashi continued to whisper "Oh no, Julie came everyday from Faridabad to Ganga Ram Hospital. She would look after the mother without a break for hours and hours, even though she got late for returning home".

"After her marriage the family turned against her. The father has not spoken a word to Julie since that day", Bhabhi provided an explanation.

Shashi's tears rolled out once again. How could a daughter not be aware of her mother's death. On one hand Pratibha cannot reach here from America in time. And the second daughter is not informed, even at the cremation of her mother. It is dreadful and Shashi could not help asking Tanvi "Beta, did you ring up Julie?"

"Yes, we telephoned. She had left for her office. We left a message".

Shashi felt that Tanvi's words were insincere. A mere formality. Didi had once confided in her. Julie came to look her one day. The father ordered everyone to stay indoors. A lock was placed on the gate. The maid servant was instructed to convey the message loudly, within hearing of the neighbours. Julie's pleading went unheeded. Angry, insulted and dejected, the girl had to leave that house; her mother's house was shut on her.

Shashi loved Julie. She stood before her eyes, 20 years younger, a girl between sixteen and eighteen. Born to parents hailing from the frontier of West Punjab (now in Pakistan) she was uncommon; extremely fair, long blonde-brown hair which she always let loose on her shoulders, round fleshy face leading to two big eyes bordered by well carved eyebrows. Not so tall but the upper and lower bodies were in harmony and the woman in her bosom was just sprouting outward. On top of it all she was courteous, laughing and vibrant, though a little open and perhaps not too measured in her conversations. To me all this was endearing, to others she was a girl to be watched.

Julie, when born, was named Jaya and was the darling of the family, being the last of four children. After she saw the film "Julie" she christened herself anew, and we all accepted her new name Julie. After all, she was a pet.

Pratibha was the eldest, no less beautiful, endowed with wisdom and soberness. Medals, certificates of merit, prizes in recitation came her way in every test and she finally cleared her M.B.B.S. examination with distinction. Suryakant happened to come to Delhi, after graduating in Enginnering at Yale University, and met Pratibha at her friend's wedding. Within days the two got married and went to the USA. Pratibha continued her medical studies to gain an M.D. in Psychiatry and got a well paying job in a hospital in Connecticut, New Jersey. Her father never failed to hail her achievements and he announced proudly, when Shashi and Ravi, called on them one day "Just look at this magazine, Shashi, on page 27 is Pratibha's photograph. Read what the professionals in America state of my daughter's brilliance and contributions to the medical profession. I knew she is the only one after me. My dream child".

"Didi, congratulations" Shashi responded with genuine pleasure. "All her achievements are due to your sacrifices for her, Didi. Read this article. Pratibha names you the inspiration and beacon in her life".

Didi's eyes were sparkling with moist beads. Obviously she was, for once, very happy and satisfied. But Rana, Didi's husband, spoke with disdain and disappointment "I wish the remaining three were a fraction of what my Pratibha does".

Sashi protested "You need not worry. In time all of them will make up. Rahul has been admitted in the Sainik School. And Julie too is studying in the tenth class, so she..."

Rana butted in, as if some raw wound had been touched "This Julie. She can never equal my Pratibha who always topped in every exam. Julie only scrapes through...". The scorn in his tone was unbearable for Julie. She stared back at her father, her eyes filled with a mixture of tears, hatred and frustration. Julie walked out.

Ravi intervened to soothen the atmosphere "Rana you are unfair. You always pick on Julie and hurt her with your taunting remarks. She is growing intolerant of you. In due time Julie will become obstinate and defiant. Mind you Rana, each of us has limitations. You ought to show regard for whatever goodness she owns".

Ravi scored a forthright response from Didi. She too, fixing her eyes on Rana said “Julie no longer listens to your admonishings. All your vibes are showing negative response. Julie need not become a doctor like Pratibha. She can join some other course of study”.

Julie returned to the drawing room with snacks and a potful of tea. With care and elegance she poured tea in the cups, extending them to Shashi, Ravi and Didi. Lastly she placed a cup for her father. There was no doubt that Julie felt hurt, her ego had been assualted in the presence of outsiders, even though they were close relatives. Shashi attempting to clear away the prevailing tension asked Julie “You must visit us at Bhopal in the summer when you get vacation”.

“Please ask my mom. I will come over if she permits”.

Ravi too softly pulled Julie to his lap and reminded her “Julie, remember Mayank. He adores you. Your name Julie Didi, Julie Didi, is ever on his lips. It is that ice cream he got from you and the trips to the market or the park. You must come and stay with us”.

“I also like him. He is a lovely child. Why didn’t you bring him today with you?”

Julie was once again her usual liveliness, carefree, laughing on everything that everyone said to her. Shashi and Ravi continued to gossip for two to three hours. No more talking of children’s competitive talents eased the mood of everyone. Rana came out with his intention to visit America, one more try at his luck, as he put it. Didi wasn’t amused. In fact she stated “You are doing well here. We get enough to live decently. What is so great in America? One visit to that country and you have gone crazy about it. It has dazzled you”.

Rana was unmoved. She was quite aware of her brother-in-law's single track mind. No one dare or could deter him from his decision, be it wrong or right. To start with, he was very hardworking, within a span of 15 years he passed examinations, through correspondence, to become a qualified Engineer. Thereafter, he specialised in Estate Evaluation. Didi spared nothing, even her ornaments were sold off, to finance Rana's studies and the schooling of the four children born in those years. The family, like everyone else, had suffered enormous losses on account of partition, India Pakistan divide, which forced them to leave hearth and home.

Rana's practice picked up gradually. His earnings grew day by day. From a rented premises they moved into a small house of their own. Pratibha became a doctor, got married and moved to America. Rahul too showed up excellence in his schooling and meritwise got admitted into Sainik School. His career was assured. Ravi and Julie the younger siblings were coming up satisfactorily. And then came the big turn in their lives. Pratibha invited her father to America. The visit was short but the effect was enormous, on Rana's mind; it was a telling one! It kindled in him a dormant desire to become rich overnight. He was ever eloquent on the rampant corruption in India. Filthy streets, pervasive diseases and inefficient governing bodies evoked criticism deep from within him. He had no respect for the Congress Party which was running the Central and State Governments. Even Nehru and Patel, the acclaimed leaders, were ruining the country was his confimed view. Everything for him came under either black or white categories. Clothes must be washed at home, by Didi. The washerwoman is unclean and may leave germs in them. The food is to be cooked at home. The dhabas and restaurants are unhygenic. He never ate Chat or Kulfi at Halwai's shop, the favourite past time with us. Didi had to give up all this and slog, to pamper to the husband's whims and fancies and, above all, odd superstitions. As it is, Rana's habits were unbearable and on top of all came the lure of America "Oh, what a country that is. Food is aplenty, without adulteration and within everybody's means. Go to any store and find for yourself everything you need. That society provides equal opportunity to one and all. Lincoln became the President, though he cut logs when he was a boy. Anyone can become rich or big there". This strain of eulogising America was countered by deprecation or ridicule for India. "This country has gone to the dogs... I hate the system here and the Government policies".

Didi would scream a protest "Here too you can contest the election. Easier said than done. Don't sit and curse others. First do something worthwhile and then cast a blame on others".

The rebuff made Rana go indoors and consume newspapers, penciling here and there. Once again tension gripped that small room. Didi was upset to the core "I can't understand this man. He is obsessed with America. Doesn't realise that it will take time to settle in a foreign land. What happens to us in his absence? The children are going astray, beyond my control. But nothing worries him. He will follow distant dreams but never be content with what is in his grasp now. I am sick of his discourses and orations, Shashi. I can bear it no longer!

Rana in the meanwhile strode out of the house, perhaps to his office. Shashi could sense that Didi was distraught and downhearted. The ogre of her husband going away on a wild goose chase, leaving her to face the hardships, was daunting for Didi who was very worried about Julie who was well near marriageable age, without the stern control of a father. Didi confided these fears of hers to Shashi who was aware of Rana's utter failure in his first attempt in the United States.

It was August 1977. Shashi and Ravi were visiting America. Since Ravi was there on official work, Shashi decided to spend 10 days with Pratibha. Rana happened to be in that country; he lived in a rented flat in New York where he was working with a firm of Consulting Engineers. It was a job secured through Suryakant's good offices. Pratibha lived in the campus of a big hospital where she held an important position. Pratibha's flat was large, fitted with all household appliances. Shashi enjoyed herself in every way and visited her brother-in-law to spend a Sunday afternoon with him. Rana glowed with satisfaction but Shashi did sense some darker feelings underneath the skin. Back with Pratibha, the real things came out of Suryakant's mouth (perhaps heart!)

"Auntie, Papa has let me down. The job which I arranged for him had enormous prospects. Had Papa stuck it out there, he would have been the Head of a Section, earning much more than he is making on his own. Papa would find fault with everyone. He framed the idea that his employer was using him for his (employer's) selfish gains. Papa fails to realise that in America the management hires and fires only for the benefit of the organisation. I pleaded with him to contain his feeling and views. But Papa is incorrigible and was asked to quit. I cannot help him any more. Let him find his own way. I have nothing to do with his jobs any more".

Shashi could gauge the intense frustration within Suryakant. She also felt sympathy for Pratibha, who sat there silently listening to her husband's bitter pourings against her father. It was apathetic, a daughter pitched between two men, each of whom mattered the most in her life. But Pratibha possessed limitless patience reinforced with the lessons from psychiatric practice on her patients. Later in the day, when Suryakant was away to his office, a letter from India arrived. Pratibha was not too happy to go over it.

"What is it, darling?" Shashi asked.

"It is Rahul's letter. Read it for yourself", Pratibha handed over the blue sheet of paper to Shashi. The letter read:

"My dearest Sister,

Please get me to the States. I promise you that I will do according to your wishes. I will do as you bid me to (do). Papa forces his own wishes on us. To meet his dreams (ambitions) we have foregone ours. Mummy never betrays her pecuniary conditions and suffers alone, crying to herself. Please call me there. Didi please.

Yours,
Rahul"

Shashi could feel the intensity of helplessness in those lines. She asked Pratibha "What have you to say to Rahul?"

"It is simply impossible Aunty. Suryakant will never agree because his efforts to rehabilitate Papa have failed miserably. He feels very badly about it".

Shashi was convinced that Rana ought to return to India and take charge of his family. His absence was playing havoc on Didi and the children who felt insulted in society and relatives. Their frustration at their plight was generating anger and hatred or severly let down. Pratibha saw a future for her brothers and sister. On many an occasion Pratibha broke down true and proper, all of which disturbed Shashi a great deal.

On returning to Delhi, Shashi called Didi on phone “Pratibha has given me a letter and a parcel for you”.

Didi answered back “I will see you tomorrow and get those articles”.

It wasn’t an easy meeting. Shashi didn’t have to talk elaborately of what she had seen in the States. Pratibha seemed to have had a long talk on phone with her mother and had given a full account of her father’s life in the States.

Soon thereafter, Shashi moved down to Bangalore as her husband had been transferred from Bhopal. But the news from Delhi was awesome. According to the letter from there, Rana had suffered a paralytic attack. Didi had rushed to America to look after him as he was hospitalised there. Julie had married Mushtaq in the Court. For this she had embraced Islam.

Oh, God, all the calamities to come on Didi. Why did Julie take this unprecedented step? It is that Rana couldn’t stand this shock? Or did he suffer the breakdown because of his own failures at work? It was a big puzzle for her. And Shashi knew that Pratibha had selected one MBA qualified boy for Julie. She was just waiting for an opportune time to have Julie travel to her and announce the arrangement formally. Why do so many woes befall on this helpless soul? Some beings come to this world to serve as well as suffer.

Shashi visited her in-laws with her children during their summer vacation. There she called on Didi who had fetched Rana to India after improvement in his health. He could lead a fairly normal life except for impaired speech. Didi joined him everywhere in his vocation of property evaluation. The earnings were adequate. Didi, when asked by Shashi, confided in her. Julie had been forbidden by Rana from entering the household. Julie pleadings were of no avail. "Rana's decision, as usual, was final".

The state of affairs at Julie's in-laws was equally disappointing. Her father-in-law was a Sessions Judge in Agra, highly educated and well respected in the community. He called Mustaq and Julie one day and was very forthright with them. "Both of you are grown up, healthy and qualified. You would have weighed the pros and cons of marrying out of your religions. Now you both go away from Agra because in this city our society will not accept you. I cannot sacrifice the rest of the family for your sake".

Julie told all this to Shashi in a chance meeting in Connaught Place. The two sat in a restaurant to exchange their tales. Julie continued "Aunty my father-in-law's stance stunned me. Mustaq Ahmed had always told me of the open mindedness of his parents and had assured me acceptance in their household. They never objected to our marrying but were not prepared to let us live under their roof. Papa has already banished me from his roof. I cannot speak with Mom and Rahul hesitatingly talks to me when I telephone. It seems he is worried that I may seek a share in the property. Perhaps this is why the gate is shut on me". Julie repeated herself a few times. In place of a lively bright-eyed Julie, the one at that time was broken and dim.

Shashi was annoyed with her. Caring little for Julie's feelings she alleged "Mind you, Julie, your affair is no credit to you. Please search within if you are blameless".

Julie could hold her tears no longer. In that restaurant, in spite of all care, her sobful crying was under many watchful eyes and raised up ears. "Aunty, you too believe that I committed a sin to marry Mustaq. Papa does not let me meet my mother. I can give my life for her. And my husband is very nice to me".

Shashi did not relent "You did commit a sin Julie, the way you conducted yourself behind the back of your parents, one of whom was struggling for his life. It is a betrayal, Julie".

Julie was not going to let Shashi leave without knowing the reality. Therefore, she poured out, "Auntie, listen to me. You are quite aware that Papa compared all of us – Rahul, Ravi and me, with our eldest sister. He wanted each of us to reach sky high in every exam, in every walk of life. I could not do well in my examinations, after which for days I was humiliated. Think of Pratibha you shameless one, I was told. Only one girl has fulfilled my dreams, and the rest of you are no good, were the words often spoken by Papa. These verbal lashings made up my mind to leave them quietly one day. And you know, auntie, that Rahul has given up his studies. He too has suffered many similar insulting remarks from Papa. He is mentally distraught, even ill. His life is in jeopardy. Auntie, he does nothing except go through books on philosophy and religion. Gives us, anyone else too, discourse on politics or whatever he freshly reads. Accepted I have a third grade brain but Rahul had been brilliant. Why he too is no longer a normal person, tell me Auntie?"

She threw up the query to me. But she was intelligent to realise that I was no insider to that family to know causes leading to such unfortunate consequences. Julie was emotionally so charged that the torrent of her anguish, hatred and rebellion boiled over.

"Papa is a dreamer, never can face reality. He has wasted his education which, for him, is only a medium of earning dollars. There is everything theoretical, rigidly ingrained notions of superior and inferior, black or white. I cannot understand the logic of his going to the USA to become rich, super rich. Once is fine. A failure is not a disaster, provided one learns from that experience. Come to think of it, there is an age to begin new adventures. Papa is past fifty, near sixty in fact. In this time to go to a foreign country, where the work culture is so different from ours. Didi and Suryakant are young, the latter studied there and knows the ways of that land. Papa cannot adapt himself to any new, different or unexpected situation. Auntie I argued, pleaded and begged of him to take care of us, the mother in particular, Her earnings were enough for us. I tried to convince him but of no avail, perhaps because a dud child was giving him some pragmatic advice. He remained adamant and intolerant, to me at least. Then one day Rahul too exploded. Papa wanted to sell off the plot in Nehru Place, the only property left with the family. The Faridabad plot had been disposed off to finance Papa's earlier trip to America. Rahul resorted to fasting against Papa's intentions; he did not take food at all for two days. Auntie, am I still to be blamed for leaving that hell? Am I responsible for his paralytic attack? A rolling stone gathers no moss, my dear one". Julie was unstoppable on that day, both in speaking and crying.

Shashi was stunned with so many revelations, the wounded inside of Julie. Still Shashi argued "Julie, you should have been patient and understanding. Your marrying Mustaq was quite a blow to your father. You should have cared for his sentiments. And you must be knowing that Pratibha had arranged a good match for you...".

Julie pounced in a flash “Pratibha, Pratibha, Pratibha. Why should I seek help from her? Haven’t we all been a burden on her? She is too good, always sending money, helping Papa in all his business ventures in the USA. Suryakant is under no obligation to our family. Papa on one hand is a strict Hindu yet on the other hand he does not hestitate to be dependent on a son-in-law, totally alien to the Indian culture and tradition. I have my self esteem, Auntie”.

Shashi was aghast. This is the same Julie whom Rana rates third rate. She was rudely awoken from her slumberous reverie by a wailing Julie, who embraced her tightly “My mom, my mom is gone. No one ever told me. They are treacherous, I am not going to forgive...” Shashi stopped Julie’s venomous outpourings on this poignant moment. She clasped Julie’s hands and took her inside the cremation ground, near the pier of her mother, where the fire was consuming the last embers of burning wood. Julie cried openly.

Rana and the others ignored her presence. But those present there, shed their tears once more, seemingly for Julie this time. Shashi pulled her away, had her wash her hands and face and the two came out together. “Could you give me a lift? I live in the Defence Colony. You can drop me on the road, after the flyover”, Julie asked.

“Yes, Julie. Come on, it is no extra effort for me. Sit in the car”. Madhav had opened the door for her and Shashi too sat along with her in the back seat. It was going to be drive of an hour. Shashi was curious to know of Julie’s life after her marriage with Mustaq.

“It is a long story, Auntie. Forsaken by parents and unwelcome among my in-laws, the times were tough.

Mustaq is simple, honest and sincere to me. His loving bond pulled me out of the abyss. I joined the American Library and worked overtime to tutor young children. Neither of us wanted to borrow money or ask for help from relatives. Mustaq joined the Law College. Two years of cold, heat, rain and my family's indifference did not deter us from our resolve to be independent. Mustaq is now practising in the Tees Hazari Courts. Like all others, he too had to struggle but now he is stabilished. We have a seven year old son who studies in Shri Ram Public School. The boy has grown in creches without the affection of grandparents. There was no Naani or Daadi to tell him stories. Baboo (her son) could not visit his uncles, and play with his cousins like all other children. Auntie, I was alone in this world, snapped from all the worldly bonds, except for the two; one of whom I had accepted and the other whom I had given birth to. These bonds only sustained me in my struggle for a respectable status in society".

They had just crossed the Parliament House. Still half an hour to go. Julie grew high in Shashi's thoughts. She had matured. It was evident that Julie had learnt the truths of life. A refrigerator, a T.V., or the brick walls do not make a home. Relationships, bonds have to be generated, nurtured, strengthened and made everlasting. There are many shocks, bitter-sweet occasions, raucous arguments and divisive issues on which families fall apart, individuals break up as nervous wrecks. This was exactly Rahul's fate. He failed to measure up to this world's cruel circumstances. Julie wanted to help her brother, especially because Pratibha could not invite him to the USA. She was helpless as Rana never let the two meet, they did talk on the phone a few times. Julie narrated the background of his plight to Shashi.

"Auntie, perhaps you don't know that Rahul qualified in the written examination of IAS. He left for interview but instead reached Sai Baba's Ashram. On reaching home he explained that he had done so to spite his father. On an earlier occasion Rahul was selected for the Military Academy. Instead of encouraging him, Papa had opined that only "Nalaiks" (low wits) opted for the Services. The intelligent ones become I.A.S. or IFS Officers. Thus belittled Rahul was hurt to the core. He girdled up to pass the IAS test but rebelled to scorn his father's wishes. I feel sorry for him but I cannot do much for Rahul, He stagnates within the walls because he did not have the courage to leave the home and become a self-made man".

What words, how true of this life which, getting warm affection grows in confidence, creativity, happiness. But sarcasm, scorn, absolute rigidity of a person's will, forcibly placed on the backs of children can ruin their lives. Only the strongest of will can survive such tortuous living. Julie was Shashi's pet. That day she had risen in her esteem.

Just then the car reached the specified place, down from the Defence Colony flyover. Madhav asked the way to Julie's house. Shashi wanted to see it herself. The car, after crossing the nullah stopped in front of a two storied house. Rehman, Julie's son was playing with another child.

"Baboo, say salaam to Naani. From today she is the Bari Maa", Julie directed her son.

Baboo was very intelligent. "Namaste Bari Maa", he said folding his hands in the correct Namaskar. But he then added "Adab Arz" raising his petite hand to his forehead. Shashi felt gratified and asked if his Dad was home.

“No, he returns home after seven or eight in the evening. Please come in Auntie and have a cup of tea” said Julie. “Not today Julie. I cannot enter your house after today’s cremation. It will be inauspicious. Some other day. I love you Julie and I am proud of you. You have built afresh a new family and Shashi moved towards the car.

“Do come some day Auntie. The old bonds have fallen apart. You may remain the only link with my parental home” Julie had tears rolling down her cheeks! ❑❑

Shiva

"Help, Nandni please help. Shiva is dying". There was desperate thumping on the door. It was two in the afternoon. Nandni had dozed off after the morning's hard schedule. There was no let up of noise on the door. Nandni hurriedly left her bed, adjusting her loose sari, she opened the door.

Malni, on the other side of the door was breathless, "Come upstairs Nandni. Shiva has throttled herself with a bed sheet. She is unconscious". The two ladies, past middle age, rushed upstairs. It was a bizarre sight. Shiva lay prostrate on the floor; a black coloured duppatta was tightly tied around her neck. Fortunately she had not hurt herself. There was no blood or injury to her head or body, though there was some froth which had oozed from her mouth.

Malni was still panting. "I am lost, Nandni. This girl was alright when I left for my school this morning. Half an hour back, the school guard came running to take me to the principal's office. It was Shiva, who in a choking voice declared, 'Mem Sahib, I don't want to live. I am killing myself. You come back soon and take over your house. And she hung up".

"Was she suffering from high fever?" Nandni asked.

"Not that, I know of. But she has been behaving strangely for the last two three days. She has been crying off and on and throwing tantrums. I could not get the name of the person she cursed".

Nandni didn't want to waste time. On the one hand she made a call to Dr. Seth, her family physician. She at the same time called her servant, Kalyan, and the maid, Pinki, for help. While Kalyan ran to fetch a glass of water, Pinki enquired in a dazed voice, "What is the matter Mem Sahib?" and continued, "She was laughing and joking yesterday evening".

Nandni paid no heed to her blabber. Instead she loosened Shiva's clothes. Kalyan and she picked up the prostrate woman to place her on a bed. Kalyan brought in the jug of water, which was splashed on the victim's face. The lifeless face twitched a little, but the woman held her eyes closed, intentionally, it seemed to those standing by. "Haa, Haa, she is feigning, Mem Sahib", chirruped Pinki.

Just then Dr. Seth walked in. After checking her pulse, the blood pressure and a few knocks here and there, assured them she was safe. A medicine was prescribed which would put her to sleep and restore her in 8 to 12 hours. Kalyan ran off to the nearby chemist's shop. Dr. Seth asked Malni to fetch Shiva to his clinic the following morning. He would make a more thorough examination and seek help of a psychiatrist too, if necessary. Dr. Seth was aware of Shiva's previous unabashedly curious behaviour on occasions...

Pinki took a chappal of hers near the nose of her seemingly unconscious friend who soon opened her eyes to everyone's relief. Surprisingly, neither the two ladies nor Shiva exchanged a word when she regained her senses. The tablet brought in by Kalyan was administered to the sick one who dozed off very soon thereafter.

Nandni came back to her flat and asked for a cup of tea. She was fagged off physically and mentally. After fortifying herself, she mused while lying down on a sofa. "Did Shiva want merely to draw attention towards her? Or was she depressed deeply to think of dying?" Two past years of Malni's stay at their house appeared sequentially on her mind's canvass.

Shiva belonged to a village near Madurai, in Tamil Nadu. Around 35 years old she is stout, dark but has inviting eyes. She had been with that household for eight to nine years. A more luxurious salary along with a free return fare to her hometown, to meet her 5 year old son, lured the woman to continue working for Malni after the transfer to Delhi of the latter's husband. The maid thought she would save enough money to send her son to a college for higher education.

Malni is a teacher at a kindergarten; she has specialised in infants' growth care. Her husband, Mahadevan, works for a multinational and had moved to Delhi on a higher position. Both of them leave for their office around 8 in the morning. Since they carry their tiffin, in hot boxes, with them, there is little of housework left for Shiva, except to clean up. Finishing her chores, she walks out with Rocky, the family's pet dog for his morning's constitutional outing. Very soon after landing at Delhi, Shiva became friendly with the dhobi family who do the colony's clothes ironing. About the same time Kalyan joined the Nandni household. Within no time they became friendly; in fact too friendly to the liking of the mistress. Just then, in the mind of the mistress rang a loud bell!

"Could it be? No it couldn't be". Nandni thoughts were rolling and rocking. But very soon a kaleidoscope runs before her eyes. The dark, stout and dark woman trots about happily and genially. Her silken skin calls for soft caresses. Kalyan was lanky, very fair belonged to the hills of Kumaon. He studied upto 8th standard at Nainital. The young boy, moving closely with the two sons of Nandni very quickly picked up urban slickness and nuances. He was very much of a dandy and a favourite of the maids, about three, working in the building. Nandni was nagged with troubling thoughts. Is he? No he cannot be. The two are of diverse ages, lineages and upbringing". Suddenly the mistress remembered.

Six months back Shiva had accosted Nandni in the lobby, when she said, "Memsahib, look at this gold chain. My memsahib has given it to me". "It is very pretty, Shiva. Is it a gift from your mistress?" Nandni showed her curiosity. The maid servant nodded her head, smiled and walked away. All the while her eyes were searching for some one else.

The full story was narrated by Malni a few days later. She has an electric sewing machine, mostly used for stitching her blouses and petticoats. Her colleagues at the school used to tell her of their miserable experiences of their tailors. Malni had learnt stitching in younger days. During her free time she gave a few lessons to Shiva who became quite proficient in sewing provided the mistress gave the cloth after cutting to her. Here was an opportunity to 'kill two birds with one stone', Malni pondered. She could relieve her colleagues from their woes and help Shiva earn some extra money. The latter relished these assignments. The additional earnings besides her monthly salary allowed her to send liberal pocket money to her son and left some savings for her. The gold pendent came from this unexpected source. Many more entertainments also followed.

One evening Shiva, Kalyan and Pinki, Nandni's casual maid-servant were off to a night show of "Pahela

Pahela Payar". Shiva was clad in a red nylon sari, powdered face and heavy red lip-stick on her lips. The gold chain on her bare front was glowing. Kalyan too was groomed for a kill. The striped T-shirt given by my son, blue jeans and liberally oiled hair made him look his best. Pinki, dressed ordinarily was no match to her companions. Alas, the contrast in their ages must have raised many eye brows in the cinema. However, within the colony it became a topic of amusement for a few weeks at least.

The light-hearted and casual get together grew into rather unpleasant absentations from their daily work. The two would steal away to the terrace as often as they could. Kalyan had to be frequently shouted for. He would appear after a gap of time giving an excuse, a new one every time. Shiva had no qualms as her mistress was at school and she would slip onto the roof top upstairs without any compunction. Nandni realised the gravity of the situation when she walked upto the terrace quietly. The two were holding hands and looking wistfully at each other.

Shiva felt guilty and her head bowed, fumbled and stuttered, "Memsahib, the kitchen was too hot and I came upstairs for a breather". Realising that was not enough to assuage me, she added, "Please don't tell my Memsahib. There is nothing serious between us. Kalyan was looking at the new ring I was wearing". Nandni was discreet and did not utter a word about this escapade of theirs to Malni. However, Kalyan was spoken to in no uncertain terms. The ironic disparities in their ages and background were highlighted. He needed the warning seriously and their meetings became few and far between.

About that time Shiva's son came over to spend his vacation. The mother in her swelled up. The five year old was pampered with treats; Pepsis, ice cream cones, chocolates and uncle-chips pouches. New clothes, a pair of jeans and a few books were purchased for him. The trips to cinema, zoo and Connaught Circus were made without Kalyan. The vacation of the boy came to end and the boy was seen off at the railway station by Shiva only. Shiva didn't speak a word with any one for days on end after her visit to the doctor. She was seen at times wiping tears from her face. Malni had informed Nandni, quite some time back that the woman had been abandoned by her husband; not uncommon among the poor strata. Either hooch, or the other woman, causes these splits. Her son was the only dear possession left with her after her broken marriage. She adored him, but at Delhi her attention got diverted.

The volcano burst one day. Right at seven in the morning, Nandni heard pounding on the front door. Shiva, sobbing profusely said, in her halting Hindi, which she had picked up in her one year's stay at Delhi, "Memsahib, you please get rid of Pinki. I do not like her". An astonished Nandni told her firmly, "Pinki has done no wrong. Where from do I get another maid? No, Shiva that is not possible".

"I will find a replacement of hers, Memsahib. She is a wicked woman", Shiva then added, "She has snatched away Kalyan from me". Without waiting for a response, Shiva walked away pouting and crying vigorously. The cat was out of the bag.

Nandni stood aghast. Life is difficult anyway and now this embroilment among the servants would add another bundle of complications. Enraged to the brim, she yelled at her help hand when he appeared "Kalyan, what is this that I hear? You ought to be ashamed of making overtures to a married woman twice your age. Further, you are reported to be flirting with Pinki also.

You too are married, you scoundrel. Sometime back you told me that your 'Gauna' (consummation of marriage) was due later this year". Hearing a loud drama going in the house, Pinki walked in. Nandni shouted at her, "And you Noorjehan (light of the world)? How could you forget your 6 month old daughter and the earning and handsome husband?" The lady of the house was unstoppable.

Kalyan dared to interrupt her, "Memsahib there is nothing the matter. We are merely good friends. Beyond gossiping, chit chatting and laughing to relieve our fatigue, there is nothing among the three of us. I know my limitations. Being the only son, I will inherit the family holding in the village whereto I shall return in a few years. My Panchayat will banish me from the village if I indulge in an illegal alliance with her or Aarti who is like a sister to me. Memsahib, if Shiva thinks I have fallen for her she is seriously mistaken. But she has been lately acting queer. Whenever Pinki comes within her sight, it seems, she becomes red and blue. She behaves queer".

Pinki chipped in, "I am happily married, madam. My husband, a driver, earns reasonably. To augment his earnings with a view to give good education to our daughter, I work only at your house. But, lately I have seen Shiva clenches her fists at me whenever I cross her path. She tries to provoke me but I ignore her. I have done no wrong. Kalyan is like my younger brother. I care two hoots for her. Let her boil and froth".

Nandni stopped her short and cautioned the two of her helps, "Enough is enough. Stay away from her".

A few days later Dr. Seth walked in to have a word with Malni and Nandni. He said, "Ladies I have observed Shiva for a week now. Medicines by themselves are not going to cure your maid. Listening to you and my own efforts to fathom her malaise tell me that another violent eruption may occur. Be watchful please, because the next attack can be more lethal. Her fixation on Nandu is somewhat deep and not uncommon. In the absence of her son, who can occupy mind and body, she is frustrated, especially since it is not engaged in household chores after madam's departure for the school".

Doctor's premonition turned true not so long thereafter. Nandni returned from the market to find her apartment wide open. Upstairs there was cacophony. Her servants were running up and down. "Nandni come up right away" she heard Malni's plea. As she reached there, a horrible sight accosted her. Shiva was prostrate and unconscious. Dark red blood was flowing from her wrist, which Kalyan was trying to bandage. Aarti was rubbing her feet".

Malni explained, "It is a bizarre situation Nandni. This woman pounced on Kalyan's throat with a sharp knife shouting, 'You have betrayed me. I will kill you. No one dare associate with you except me". She had seen him carrying your bag upstairs helped by Pinki. The sight of the two together is anathema to her, as you know. Kalyan was quick and smart. He freed himself from her hold. I held back Shiva firmly in my arms. 'O.K., I will kill myself' and Shiva cut her wrist in no time. While I ran to call the doctor, the boy and Pinki helped Malni attend to the unconscious Shiva".

The Doctor's foreboding came true. He administered a sedative to her. And a psychiatrist was called in who culled out startling facts. Shiva was born in a middle class family of nine members. Her father owned a few acres of rich paddy fields and the family had no care in the world. Shiva, the lone sister of six brothers was a pampered and playful child. An uncle of hers, without children, came over from Madras (Chennai) and took the lovely child to his home. A few days later a catastrophe visited the family. All the seven were found dead in their beds, their bodies had turned black and blue. A vigorous investigation found that they had died due to food poisoning. It turned out that a lizard had fallen into the 'sambhar' which all of them partaken the previous night. The poisonous reptile had fallen from the roof into the boiling broth when the lady had gone to the bathroom to relieve herself.

Shiva was brought up by the kind uncle, but the trauma had left her bitter and of a skewed mind. She was duly married off when she was sixteen to Ramalingam, from the same community. He was twenty years her senior; no one considered this match-making anything queer, new or uncommon. The husband gave nothing more than abuses and beatings after booze sessions with friends and playtime with other women. Hardly anytime was available for Shiva who had to wait for 14 years to get a son from her man. She got happy days for once in her troubled days. But this relief was not to last. Ramalingam could brook no un-attention from his wedded slave, who naturally spent more of her time with the new born. As a result she was booted out. Shiva moved from one household to another, working day and night for her child and herself. Ultimately, she found permanent place with Malni and came over to Delhi leaving the child to the care of her uncle whom she compensated for the boy's upkeep and education. Shiva, however, remained physically unfulfilled. Hence her infatuation for Kalyan!

The psychiatrist further cautioned that Kalyan or Pinki should never appear in her vicinity. He wanted Malni to be around Shiva for fifteen days at least, even if that means her taking a break from the school. After she gets to her normal behaviour she should be dispatched, accompanied by someone to Madras. Malni observed diligently the doctor's advice administering tablets and mixtures. Her devoted and affectionate care of Shiva was rewarded; she gained complete health sooner than expected. Nandni was only too pleased to see Shiva when she came to say good-bye. "Memsahib, it was my fault. Please forgive me for my outbursts and unbecoming behaviour". Shiva touched Nandni's feet who blessed her from the core of her heart. The latter gifted a shawl and also gave her a hug, as happens when two friends part company. Malni herself escorted the chastened girl to Madras and assigned to the care of one of her friends.

Kalyan too left to his village very soon thereater. Before going away he once again assured his mistress of his good intentions. He had never behaved indecently towards neither of the maids. He befriended Shiva only because he found no one else as honest and sincere as her! Nandni believed him.

Nandni receives letters from Malni off and on. These letters mention that Shiva no longer gets tantrums. Much of her time is spent in looking after Ranga, the name she has given to her son. She confirms that Shiva's leaning towards Kalyan was a genuine one. She was looking for someone to be by her side to help her forget her lone, solitary thirty long years. It is a pity that she betted on a wrong person.

Nandni cannot stand lizards and hates them whenever she sees them crawl on the wall. She is reminded of the tragic deaths of Shiva's parents and six siblings! ❑❑

Girls Don't Cry

1. It happened at Solan

"Daadi, come out of your room and see who is come", Dayanand's joyous and sonorous voice echoed, in the courtyard of a bungalow at Solan. The happy couple had returned from the District Hospital.

"Who is it? My back is aching and I cannot get up". The old lady had given up hope of any thing good happening in the family.

"It is a 'Lakshmi', Daadi, Lakshmi", Dayanand tried to lure her. Kulwanti stood by his side, holding a live and kicking bundle in her hands, hoping to be welcomed ceremoniously, with '*Kumkum and Aarti*' (traditional Hindu ritual). "From where has she come?" Daadi was reluctant to move from her cozy abode. "Oh, Daadi, you are a limit. Kulwanti has delivered a baby girl", Dayanannd went to her room and tickled her bones. Both laughed. "They are waiting for you at the door", giving her a hint.

"What a dud I am! I should have known better", she mumbled. In no time, Daadi darted like a dear, on her spindly legs, with a decorated plate in her hands to welcome the grand daughter. The baby's arrival had pumped tons of energy into her. She put 'a tilak of kumkum', on the mother's as well as the child's foreheads. Sprinkling rose petals on the threesome, and holding a lighted lamp in front of them she led Kulwanti to a well arranged bed. Daadi squatted comfortably on the bedside and pulled away the child into her lap. The old lady kissed the newborn's forehead, twirled round a silver coin over the child's body, to be given in charity to the maid, attending on the household. She got up straightened her bow-like waistline and performed a jig, and chanted, again and again, "Jug Jug Jeo my child, (May you live long). Thank you, O, Lord, You have bestowed this precious gift to us. Daya what have you named her?"

"That is for you to decide, Daadi", Dayanand said out of respect for his grandmother. "I will call her CHAMKO. Think of it, a child is born in our family after 35 years! The girl has brightened not only these four walls but shooed off darkness from our family", said the wrinkle-laden grandmother. Daadi's heart was brimming with joy. She beckoned the servants to bring 'Ladoos' to be freely distributed to visitors to the bungalow.

Surprisingly her bronchitis and arthritis were no where around till late in the evening when the latent maladies returned with a vengeance. She had to be repaired to her bed and given a sedative.

* * *

Raaj Raani, Dayanand's grandmother was 87, the sole surviving member of the earlier two generations. For more than fifty years, she ruled over the seven room bungalow-estate, called Preet Villa, a legacy from her husband who retired as Civil Surgeon of the City Hospital. They had a son and a daughter, the former, was a commissioned officer in the army and the latter, was studying at Delhi, to be a doctor. Amar Anand, on becoming a Captain, was married to Kalyani, who gifted a son, a year latter. Those were golden years.

Then a slew of tragedies visited the household. Nandita while riding on her cycle was knocked down by a D.T.C. bus. The son died in the war with Pakistan, in 1965. Kalyani, his wife, took to living in an Ashram at Hardwar, leaving the child to Raaj Raani's care. The Civil Surgeon, shocked and depressed, by the two unexpected and untimely deaths, could not survive a heart attack. God's wrath had visited the family, thought the unlucky lady.

Devoid of interest in this world Raaj Raani stayed in bed, in one of the seven bed rooms in Preet Villa whom she termed as 'Ateet Villa' (The abode of the past). From its window she could see 'Pine' and 'Deodar' trees on the distant hill-slopes which were snow clad in winters and rains washed them in monsoons. The air was salubrious the year round. In fact, it was highly rejuvenating and rich in oxygen. A lawn girdled the house, but the old lady cared little for all the beautiful gifts of nature because of bitter memories of the past. Over the years she was reduced to a skeleton of bones, each one of them aching and stiff. Her chest rattled continuously and eyes were going dim day by day.

* * *

A long toil followed. Dayanand, whom the old lady had to bring up, waiting patiently for sunny days. He received the utmost care and attention of Raaj Rani. She left no stone unturned to give him the best education. Dayanand built up a lucrative practice after obtaining a degree in Ayurveda from Agra University. Solan in the past few years has been a hub of industrialisation, particularly of electronic manufacturing supplying goods to major telecom companies. But in the days when Vaid Dayanand set up his shop, a bazaar, one kilometer long, played host to tourists on their way to Shimla, the capital of the Government of Himachal

Pradesh. Mostly, eating joints, a few posh restaurants, and tea stalls for the bus-drivers did a roaring business. Those suffering from hill-sickness found a messiah in the Vaid. The local population suffering from malaria or gastronomic ailments reckoned his pills extremely effective. The Vaid's earnings were handsome. Dayanand earned the title of 'Vaidraj' from his fraternity. But his material and professional achievements gave rise to resentment among the medical fraternity, particularly, those practicing the other Indian medical systems. One medic, Rudra Dev was extremely jealous of him. By one means or another, this evil man wanted to decimate his rival.

Dayanand, and his wife, Kulwanti had everything except a child, though they were married for ten years. His medicines cured ailments of thousands but his wife's pregnancy eluded him. Legend has it that a Sadhu came to their house and gave a pinch of 'Dhooni' (white powder), each to the duo. A few matrimonial tricks, as advised by the sage were also adopted. When the lady's 'periods' were due, they held their breath. Soon after the passage of two more months, the couple became hopeful. Dayanand talked to no one of the coming delightful days. Wanti appeared rarely in the town or the neighbourhood. Lest someone should..., she shuddered even to think of the... . This secret was not shared even with Raaj Raani for upto the fifth month of pregnancy. Her interest in life bounced back, knowing that Kulwanti would deliver a child some day. And then the miracle happened!

2. Chamko is different

The baby's arrival pumped tons of energy into the trio, Raaj Raani, Dayanand and Kulwanti. Within 24 hours of the child's birth, Kulwanti's parents arrived from Delhi. The father got busy in announcing its arrival to all and sundry. Pujas and Havans happened on one pretext or another. Every one, living in Solan, attended one or more of those festive occasions. They congratulated the happy family and were rewarded with rich delicacies. The house and the neighbourhood were transformed. Everyone slobbered over the baby and made strange gestures, noises and faces, as if they had gone to their own 'puppy' days. Ladies were very particular. Curling of lips, a yawn or a smirk was noticed and commented upon by them. At times Chamko warbled, made faces and occasionally giggled, perhaps, at their stupid endeavour to teach her a number of human languages. The baby must have thought (if it could do so), it had descended into a loony world. Leaving aside the common beings, even the wise, the old and the young were un-inhibited in their wayward, baby-like, theatrical expressions. They vied with each other to gain control of the infant. Except the person in whose lap Chamko rested, every one else sulked, even if the kid wetted the holder or was doing potty. Wanti, however, found nothing sweeter than sleeping at night with her baby and feeling her warm breath on her cheek. Raaj Raani accepted this superior right of the mother, only because she was afraid of passing over her bronchitis to the child. Babies are such a wonderful gift of God and must be preserved at all costs!

In a few months the first major achievement of Chamko caused a shout-for-shout row among the three guardians. The girl uttered her first word 'a...a'. "Listen", Raj Raani called everyone around to her bedside, and declared, "She is calling me, 'Ba', meaning 'Badi Maa' (the senior mother)". The others were not convinced and sniggered.

Wanti couldnot have it and said, "She very clearly said 'Ma'. Dayanand, shaking his head negated them and instead staked his own claim, "It was 'Pa'. She is Papa's girl".

The fight was only settled with the arrival of a team of expert linguists, consisting of grandmotherly neighbours. They, being very judicial minded waited to hear the child speak again, which took a few hours. Their verdict in favour of 'ma', was, however, more based on tradition than on phonetic sciences. The defeated papa and grandmother went into a sulk. Even otherwise, the changing of diapers and staying up nights made the parents cranky. Stress levels were going up and the once happy parents would fight and cuss at the drop of a feather. The wife roared at her husband when a feeding bottle, a bit too hot, was placed in Chamko's mouth and she gave a loud yelling out of distress.

"You will never learn. Now you have scalded my kid's delicate tongue", such tongue-lashings were common for Dayanand. He generally floundered in his parental desire to help. Then one afternoon without warning, the baby stood up and took her first little step, wobbling and fell down. It was one giant step which put the 'Ba', 'Ma' and 'Pa' in a tizzy. The three hugged and kissed the child and went shouting, "Soon there will be something bigger to look forward to. Any day now our precious one will walk, and go to school", declared Dayanand.

However, there was one issue of concern. The little one did not talk for months. "Is she going to talk at all? Not relying on his own medical intelligence, an allopathic Doctor was consulted. "Is she likely to be dumb?" the parents and Raaj Raani were very worried. "It will happen in time, she is hardly 10 months old", the Doctor tried to smother their nervousness. She learnt to totter and titter about a bit. She would tug at her mother's dress when she wanted to be fed. "She is 'too-oo', intelligent", Wanti would say confidently. The parents were swooning. Papa would be busy doing 'coochie-moochie', while the mother filled up the feeding-bottle. Chamko reached out for the bottle, which slipped, fell, and broke into pieces. Chamko was rock-like silent for a few seconds and then went into a long spell of crying, tears flowing down her eyes. Wanti and Dayanand were surprised. The parents picked her up and feigned to be crying, raising a mini-storm in the room. They also pretended to play 'ouie-ouie', as if they were seriously wounded. It took a while to mollify the child?

In her time, the girl learnt to talk and walk. She would hold her father's finger to move around the family lawn. Dayanand collected a parrot, 2 sparrows, a dog and a lamb for her to play about. When Chamko was 4-5 years old the father would walk her upto hill tracks, laced with terraced corn or wheat fields. Simple walks with her father around the bazaar, or the 'pugdandis' on summer evenings did wonders for her, which she remembered and recounted when she was an adult.

Chamko was a precocious child. The growing girl learnt fast to distinguish between the voices of koels, sparrows, crows, parrots and a host of other birds. She could differentiate between vegetables: potatoes, carrots, peas and cauliflower. Many a 'Jari-Booti', (herbal and medicinal plants) became known to her. Vaid Ji acquainted her with the properties and uses of Basil, Haldi, Garlic, Chandan, Rose, Coriander, Mint, Clove, and many more plants. She also knew that Aakleaves' milk, which Dayanand obtained from Rajasthan, is very effective in curing boils. While making medicines, the father taught the daughter how to extract juices from the herbs and minerals: sulphur, zinc, iron and copper. She could recognize the different tree roots and the beneficial or harmful effects of their extracts. Furthermore, the girl was taught many simple, natural and cheap recipes like: to rub the teeth with mixture of lemon and orange peels, after the daily cleaning of the teeth with 'Meswalk datun'. The teeth remain milk white. Honey, ground ginger and a pinch of black pepper in hot water, cure sore throat. Chamko was given lessons in personal and civic hygiene too. At a very early age, she knew that the 'ornamental fish', if put in drains, eat up mosquito larvae, preventing breeding of malarial mosquitoes. (See Note at the end). Her father taught her many a rhyme to sing and remember naturopathy:

(i) A few morsels less than your fill,
Two liters of water to top the till,
Three times walking, living honky-dory,
Enjoy hundred years healthy and happy.

(ii) Drink a few liters of water every morning
Doctors stay away, is wise sages' warning

By the time Chamko was 14 years old she was a versatile operator. She had completed her matriculation and was a full fledged curator of a number of maladies and produced posters on disease prevention and their curses by natural plants and herbs. At curing snake-bites she had gained proficiency, which made her well-known in Solan and towns nearby.

Off and on, the housewife, Wanti, would have wordy duels on her score with her husband. "Chamko is not learning the house-hold chores", she would complain. No one would marry the budding "Miss Medicine", was her constant refrain. The father was adamant and keen to leave with her the legacy of his medical knowledge. Chamko accompanied him on visits to patients' homes and his tours of hospitals. 'She would become a famous

Vaid in her own right', Dayanand would dream, 'and he could enjoy his retirement surrounded by his grandchildren'. But he did not live to see that day.

3. A Grievous Blow

Raaj Raani fell ill seriously. The family made their way to Delhi for her treatment. Dayanand also collected herbs and powders for the shop. While returning from Delhi, the bus was waylaid, a few kilometers before Solan. Bullets were showered on it from all directions. The occupants went helter-skelter to save their skins. Vaid Dayanand and his wife Wanti were frisked away by the marauders, leaving behind the scared, Raaj Raani and Chamko. Police reached the site and escorted the shaken men and women to Solan in their vans. Six gun shots were heard, a little after the police contingent disappeared. The dead bodies were recovered a few days later. The old woman, Raaj Rani, could not withstand this onslaught of tragedies and passed away a week later.

Chamko's world was shattered to pieces. The neighbours came in ones and twos to commiserate with her. After a few days of sympathetic stories by do-gooders, all of them took to their routine. A strange life descended on Chamko. Lonely and forlorn she had the company of a parrot, a pigeon, a lamb and a few squirrels. Her childhood friend Lajwanti, nicknamed affectionately 'Lajo', came to live with her a few times, but had to return to her home to help her mother. The life was dull and meaningless for the unfortunate survivor.

Champakali commenced practicing medicine from the house itself. This had to be stopped because the authorities insisted on seeing a license with her. In the bazaar, Rudra Dev's practice, of the 'unani' system of medicines, picked up. Till Vaid Dayanand was alive, the Hakim had paltry income. He wanted to rule the domain after the death of his rival. And now this girl was a thorn in his flesh. 'I am not letting this chip of a girl to rob me of my due, any more', he vowed to himself...

A few days after Vaid Dayanand's demise, a hard knock startled Chamko. A young man, well built, fair, dressed in light grey bush-shirt suit, carrying a black suitcase stood at the door. Alongside was a sixty odd years' old skinny but alert eyed woman. Carrying a 'Jhola' on her shoulders, she smiled and said, "Can we come in? Pity you don't recognise us. Never mind, I am your father's Chachi and Jogi is my son". Without ado the pair walked in.

Lajo, who had temporarily moved in with Chamko, went inside to fetch water for them to drink. The old woman wailed and cried, "How could Almighty be so cruel to take away my nephew?" On the other hand, Jogi consoled her, "Don't you worry, sister. I shall take care of you". The intense grieving when softened, the boy took to easy talking, as if he had been, for years, a close friend of the family. The girls offered them a decent dinner and put them up in Vaid Ji's room which had been locked till then. The two thugs folded up in the room and bolted the door from inside.

The following morning, Jogi tried to be formal and friendly at the same time, "Champa Ji, forgive me if I don't call you Chamko; it sounds boorish", On one pretext or another he would indicate his own deep interest in medicinal matters. To the extent he ventured to tell her, "Sister I know how to prepare a powder from dead scorpions. It is so effective a remedy against poisonous pest bites", and paused to see the impact of his revelation.

"Is it so? I would like to learn the recipe. But how do you manage to catch scorpions? Their bite causes excruciating pain", queried Champakali "Ah catching scorpions is easy for me. I managed to procure pills which emanate a scent to attract scorpions in a wire net. Then they are left in the hot sun, to dry and harden up. In two days they die of hunger and I mill them into fine powder. Champa Ji, it is a problem to gather four or five of them at a time. To get to their underground habitat is so dangerous", Jogi showed his manly prowess as well as mastery over curing poisonous bites; snakes excluded because he knew Champakali was good at that.

"I don't know how I shall manage all that much on my own", Chamko inadvertently expressed her helplessness.

"I will not let you perform that dangerous pursuit. It is a man's job", Jogi was chivalrous and added a soother, "You are not alone anymore. We are going to live together from now on".

The plan was getting unfolded. The old woman, though frail and rickety, took charge of the household affairs. A maid was taken on, and Lajo was repatriated to her own home.

The following day, Jogi made advances. He asked, "Have you been to Delhi?" Champa started crying instead of answering the question. Realising his mistake he made a quick about-turn, and said, "I am very sorry. I meant Shimla. Have you ever been to Shimla?"

"No", was her abated reply.

"It is a great place. We must go there", Jogi had hit on a trail to win her over. "You have never seen a place like that Champa. You cannot imagine the grandeur of the Vice-regal lodge. It is majestic. What a fine building GHQ is, six stories tall! And the Ridge! In evenings it is full of town's gentry. The military and police bands play to entertain the public. Come on Champa, we will go their tomorrow itself", Jogi was informal and excited. "But I don't have the money", Champakali showed her reluctance.

"Main Hoon Na (I am there to take care of it all)", Jogi reassured her. "Can Lajo come with us?" the girl asked.

"Don't be silly. I am leaving my mother behind. Only the two of us will have a good time", Jogi was feeling very elated. He had won over Champakali, he thought. He spent the rest of the day in planning and making arrangements for the trip to Shimla. Their bus would leave at nine in the morning, the following day, he announced. To his mother he virtually ordered, "Mother, please make sure that we have 'Aloo Poori and Halwa in sufficient quantity. I want Champa to have fun and forget her grief. We would be away for three days".

Jogi and his mother disappeared in the evening for a number of hours, on the pretext of buying provisions. Strangely, Chamko's parrot kept on repeating, "Matt Jana, Matt Jana" (Don't go, don't go). The lamb and the squirrel jumped into her lap and wouldn't think of leaving. Lajo was skeptical about the fancy sojourn to Shimla. However, the naive girl had fallen for Jogi's glib talking. Lajo had no choice but to help her friend pack the clothings and other paraphernalia, including the medicine kit that she would need in the following two days.

As Jogi and Champa were leaving the house a snake came up with his hood upright. It was shooed off, with a long stick, by the young man. The owl on the tree top screeched. The parrot was repeating the earlier warning, "Matt Jana". A thought crossed Champa's mind. Are these friends warning me against a likely mishap? Never believe in superstitions, her father had said. She walked along the newly acquired friend. A grandmother and a brother cannot be cheats! Lajo and Chachi saw them off well secured in the bus, en route to Shimla.

Lajo went to see the house the day after her friend's departure. The gate and the doors, of the bungalow, stood ajar. Inside there was an eerie silence. There was not a thing left there, nor the birds and the lamb. All the household furniture and other belongings were missing. A chill went up her spine and a frantic cry rang within her body. Was it a robbery or a nefarious plan by con-thugs? A worried Lajo left the bungalow. She was confused.

The matter was reported to the Kotwali at Solan, who rushed a police party to Shimla to track Champakali and Jogi. Only one clue came their way from the Transport Company's driver. A young man and a girl had gone out at Tara Devi halt, 15 kilometers before Shimla to visit the Keventer's Milk Plant, the most modern dairy set-up to meet demand of dairy products from the Chief Minister's and Governor's households and other establishments. They did not return, though the driver waited for them, much after the scheduled departure from there. All the police stations in Himachal State were put on alert to track the fugitives.

In the meantime, Champakali while touring the plant asked one of the guides, "Where are these cows from? They look very different from our hill-stock".

"They are 'Jersey' cows, imported from an island called Jersey, near England", said the Officer and added, "They deliver nearly 30-40 liters of milk, as against only 7-10 liters by the local breeds".

"Why don't we import more for the entire country or reproduce more of their kind in India?" was her next query.

"This genre survives only in cold climate. Therefore only a few locations can host them. Moreover, we have imported enough numbers to supply to a select numbers of customers in Shimla and Delhi".

Moving around them, they saw machines milking the cows into rubber pipes filling directly huge vats inside the building.

"What is happening in those big vessels, Sir?" was her next inquiry.

"We are pasteurizing the milk?" was the brief reply.

"Why are you doing all this? I know nothing about pasteurizing", was another one from Champakali.

The officer was indeed surprised, and pleased, at her investigative stance. He replied, "Pasteurizing means raising the temperature to very high temperature for about 4 minutes. This process kills almost all bacteria, which if not destroyed, can cause indigestion or discomfort. We also take care to ensure that the milk is collected from healthy cows only. You should know that our hill cows sometimes suffer from tuberculosis".

As they moved along, they reached the 'Cold Room', where the treated milk is reduced to virtually freezing temperature. They also saw the bottling and packing of bottles for dispatching to distribution points.

Jogi was getting impatient, "Champa let us go. We will be late for Shimla", he said.

"Oh, it is so interesting. I can spend days here".

"Some other time", he said and made a move to quit. Inwardly he was pleased that his attempt to impress Champakali was working. They caught the train to Shimla from Tara Devi. Jogi had maneuvered to give a slip to the police. 'In case the Solan Police had sent a wireless message to intercept them at the bus terminal?' At Shimla, he went into a friend's house below the railway station. They were safely lodged there for the night and a few days' picnicking.

4. Sightseeing at Shimla

The morning was bright and sunny. Looking out of her window, Chamko saw hundreds of houses on a hill slope. Their roof tops, painted white, red, blue or green made the town colourful. Shimla was massive for the girl from the nondescript Solan. She was awe struck by the tall cedars, thick forests of pine and flowering shrubs. It was a magnificent setting of high peaks, rising one on top of the other till she could see traces of snow-clad line of a mountain-range far off across the north. Excited she asked, "Where are we going now?" "You wait and see. Come with me", Jogi teased her.

Winding up bye-lanes they reached the shopping Mecca of Shimla, the Lower Bazaar, just above the 'Subzi Mandi (vegetable market)'. At a halwai's shop they had breakfast of 'Puri-Aloo, Chat and jalebees'. A kilometer or more of shops of provisions, woolens, shawls, Himachal's distinctive caps, jams and squashes, lined on either side, were tempting. But the best were silver jewellery establishments, tinklets for the feet, multi-laced necklaces and broaches and clips for the hair. Jogi asked, "Do you want any of them?"

Champakali was embarrassed and coyly answered, "Those are for married women. What can I do with them?"

"You can get married", a hint was thrown to her.

"Dhut, don't tease me. Not yet". Jogi knew that he needed to keep trying for a while. The Mall, virtually the upper deck of the Lower Bazaar, was a class by itself. The famous restaurants Davicos, Wengers and a few European style wine shops brought back to Chamko's mind lessons in pre-independence history.

"See Champa, this is called Scandal Point", Jogi was loud, excited and emphatic. "What does that mean?" Chamko was blank.

"Nearly eighty years ago, the British Commander-in-Chief's daughter eloped with the Maharaja of Patiala. Since then the young lovers meet here". Jogi watched keenly for Chamko's reaction. "The Maharaja was characterless. And these young brats are shameless. There are better things to do than make a public exhibition of their deepest emotions". Champakali was clear and blunt. Jogi's hopes received a setback. Dejected, he asked, "Where shall we go now?"

"You name them, I will choose". "We can go to Summer Hill", said Jogi and added, "On the way we will see Cecil Hotel, Viceregal Lodge and at the end will go to the hill top where Mahatama Gandhi held his prayers.

"And where else can we go?"

Jogi replied, "To Chhota Shimla, to see the majestic building Ellerslie, which houses the offices of the Government of Himachal. From there we can go to

Barnes Court, erstwhile Governor's Lodge, and presently the Rajbhawan".

"Why do you talk of big people and big buildings only? Are there no temples in this city?" Champakali's voice was somewhat stern. "Of course there are. The Kali Bari is quite near. Finally we shall visit Jakoo, the Hanuman's temple", and the schemer quickly changed his stance and also planned his final move.

Kali Bari was reached in just ten minutes. A black marble image of goddess Kali is flanked by vermillion daubed stone carvings. Champa prostrated in front of the sanctum, meditated for a few minutes and donated a waft of her hair.

"Did you make a wish?" was her companion's inquiry.

"I never ask for favours. Gods and goddesses have so far been kind to me. I believe they will always remain my guardian angels". Firmness, self confidence and faith echoed from her words.

Jogi could make out nothing and beckoned her towards Jakoo. The Hanuman temple is on a 2800 meters high peak and is a strenuous trek. Before taking the climb, he saw that Champakali takes a decent lunch. En route he purchased roasted horse-gram, peanuts, laddoos and a pair of yellow-marigold garlands. Chamko guessed that the laddoos and the 'malas' (garlands) were for offerings at the altar, but the bag of horse-grams was a mystery and therefore questioned, "What are the grams and peanuts for?"

"There are hundreds of hanumans on the way", said Jogi and laughed. At that moment, the joke and the laughter fell flat on Chamko. But soon the mystery unfolded itself. On either side of the trek were groups of monkeys, hundreds of them, as Jogi had indirectly hinted. Chamko was amused and she freely distributed their favourite foods. Soon after, the clever pigmy-gods wrested away the bag from her hand.

The scenario from top of the hill was gorgeous. Thousands of roof tops were a colourful huge umbrella, giving shelter to a massive humanity. White clouds hovered over distant hill ranges, some of them even higher than the peak she stood upon. On Westside, a setting sun gave way to darkness. It began raining. The duo went in to pray and offer their homage to Lord Hanuman. Champakali repeated her act of meditation and prayers. She was astonished when she raised her head and opened her eyes. Jogi said, "We will marry here and seek God's blessings", and moved forward to garland Champakali. Like a stroke of lightning she withdrew herself. Deeply annoyed she pouted with anger, "You rascal! You said I am your sister. Do sisters wed their brothers in India?" The combatant in her came to the fore.

Chamko ran fast down the hill. Jogi caught with her after a gallop and dragged her into a standing 'riksha' (a four men pulled hand-cart, common in Shimla) and bade them to his friend's house. He knew by then that Champakali was no ordinary nut to crack. The girl had taken advantage of his soft and friendly approach. 'Nothing but wily and stern ways will work', thought Jogi.

5. A Rock Melts

Champa was drowsy. Her head was spinning like a top. The eyes would open for some moments and thereafter drown in nothingness. At last she gained her wits and found herself in a strange place. Where was she? Jogi and she were going to Shimla, flashed in her mind. But that room was not the same that she occupied in Shimla. How did she reach in that room?

Her thoughts and head were spinning fast, reaching no definite conclusion.

"Here is a hot cup of coffee for you, dear", Chachi walked in.

Champa smothered the questions arising in her mind. Without signs of nervousness she sipped the drink to shake off the heaviness on her head. The old woman stroked her hair to speed up the process of her return to normalcy. Chamko took full control of her senses and walked into the W.C. to wash herself. Were Jogi and Chachi fakes? There and then she resolved to unravel the mystery. She would show no tantrum nor do anything in haste..

The old woman was able and efficient. She had already readied a few vegetables, perhaps, anticipating her arrival. The chappatis were baked in no time. The three of them had a hearty meal and sound sleep afterwards. What else could one ask at that strange place!

Looking out of the window, the following morning, she realised that the hutment was perched on a steep slope of a hill. Surrounded by a thick jungle it would hardly be visible from a distance. The sun was fresh, bright and warm. Cool breeze stroked her cheeks. Champa felt exuberated and wanted to have a long walk. But the room was locked from outside. Jogi was missing. The girl looked askance at the old woman, who gave a crooked smile. Champa had been tricked and trapped. Clever as she was, she showed no emotion; instead pretended that she would gladly accept her fate.

"How should I address you?" she queried, but answered herself, "I am so stupid to be asking this. Being my father's Chachi, you are my Daadi and I shall address you so".

The woman nodded her ascent. And then an accident took place. While cutting the 'Palak leaves', she cut her thumb, blood flowing out of it. Champa was quick to hold the finger tight and place it under the cold water of the tap. The loss of blood stopped. Soon a poultice was applied on the sore thumb. It burnt for a while but was soothing thereafter.

"From where did you get that poultice?" the woman asked.

"Daadi there are Haldi pieces in the kitchen. I have Multani Mitti and Chandan in my suitcase. I made a past of these ingredients and put it on your wound", replied the girl.

A friendly chord struck inside the old witch. Why need she do harm to a good soul? One deed doesn't prove goodness of a creature, the thought jumped in her mind. 'After all I shall receive a handsome booty from Jogi, when he marries her', overwhelmed her mind. Forget the damned thought! Daadi returned to her nasty ways. She made Chamko slog the whole day, in cleaning the house, washing clothes and cooking food for six persons. In the evening Jogi returned with his friends.

"Where are the bottles, man?" one of them asked.

"Don't be in a hurry. Beer is nice only when cold. I have put them in the stream to cool", answered Jogi. Sloan's Dyer Meaking Brewery was famous for its beer. The waters of the streams were as pure and healthy as those in Scotland, even to the extent of containing similar minerals. (The Brewery thrives till today). The fellow wanted to celebrate the booty he had struck, and a young girl for himself!

"I hope we will have something to eat with our drinks", said another man.

"Plenty man, plenty", and Jogi shouted, "Chamko where are the 'Pakoras'?"

They celebrated the whole evening with beer from Solan brewery and enjoyed the snacks followed by hearty meals.

One of them popped up the question, "When do you propose to marry her. I cannot wait to taste a beauty like her". All of them laughed and individually passed lecherous remarks. The rascal opened his cards, "Let her ripen, man. Slowly and steadily I shall devour her and her belongings. I would marry the beautiful girl after she gets used to the new environment. Where is the hurry? Let the girl come round, which is bound to happen one day", he added.

The celebrations went on till late in the night. Champa got disgusted with their demeaning remarks about her; the longer they continued the more bitter she became. That evening she vowed to escape from that den, and teach a lesson or two to that braggart. The fight was on, but in her way and on her terms. Her face and manners, outwardly, must stay calm and sober!

The day that followed was a bad one for the old woman. Either it was over eating or some thing, in the previous evening's dinner, that had not suited her. Vomiting and loose stomach was killing. On the other hand, heavy work and a late night were also taking their toll. Her bones and flesh were giving way. "I am dying, my child. Save me from the 'Yamraj' (devil who carries the dead to hell or heaven)", she beseeched and wailed.

"Nothing to worry, Daadi, I am here to look after you", Champa consoled her. She squeezed an onion and half a lemon and gave her a spoonful of the juice every five minutes or so. It took nearly an hour or so to stop those obnoxious pourings, from her both ends, resulting in dehydration. The angel had an answer for that too.

"Daadi drink this", the girl advised.

"What are you giving me now? I have hardly stopped excreting. Will the old routine not start again", Chachi expressed her doubt. She wanted to be certain now whatever she was going to eat or drink. The previous night's nasty experience cannot be endured again, she thought. Champa explained to her, "Daadi, you have lost a great amount of fluid from your body. To compensate that loss, I am giving you nothing but boiled water with lemon juice and sugar and a pinch of salt". Chamko made certain that Chachi did not suffer from dysentery.

"Why do you add both, sugar and salt, my dear?"

"Grandma, the sugar will restore energy to your body, and the salt has sodium in it, which is an essential ingredient in your body-fluid", the girl clarified. Champa plucked a few ripe pomegranates from the orchard and asked Chachi to chew its seeds.

"Daadi, there is a saying, 'Sau Beemar, Aik Anaar – A pomegranate can cure one hundred patients/ ailments". And they both had a hearty laugh.

It seemed that old woman had not one but one hundred ailments. If it was headache one day then arthritis appeared with a vengeance the following day. She had high blood pressure and diabetes too. Champa realised medication only was not the answer. Budia's (the old woman's) diet would have to be managed. It is difficult to teach an old woman to dance, goes the saying. The job was not an easy one in this case. But she was patient and perserved. 'One cannot turn a heart in one day', She understood very well! The living regime of the woman required changing.

The diet was made more soothing and agreeable, using more leafy vegetables, pulses, lesser fat and spices. One day she chanced to see, at the back of the hut the plant 'Ispagul' (Plantago Ovata) plant she milled the upper part, sieved and winnowed the seeds and cleared them of all pests and dust. The husk so obtained is called Sat-Isabgol, she informed Daadi. The purified output was administered daily to the old lady, with sugar, in a glass of water. At times she would get milk and honey, through Jogi, to enhance the effect of the potion. Within a month Chachi was rid of her constipation and the impact of diabetes and high blood pressure was also lessened. Chamko was confident that given time that she would cure all the ailments of her adopted grandmother.

Daadi was impressed and felt assured, "May God bless you", came out from within her heart, voluntarily. Now the old woman had no doubt that Champa could do nothing wrong, at least would do no harm to her. She on her part would see no harm done to her. Jogi's evil designs must not succeed and would be foiled, became her resolve.

One fine day Jogi appeared out of the blue. The man was treated ceremoniously with good food. both Daadi and Chamko wanted to please him, each with a different motive. He was on his own for a few hours, during which he presumably drunk himself to punk state. Early in the morning Chamko heard a rumpus going on in the room next to her. She heard:

"What are you upto, Jogi?" the old woman asked.

"Just a little play and fun! After all such occasions don't come every day", Jogi was loose in his talk about Champakali.

"Beware young man, you cannot touch her", the woman was defiant! Jogi was agog and said, "You are going to get your money. What makes you so attached to that cat?"

"She is not a cat, Jogi. She is a decent girl. From now on she is a good as my grand daughter. And don't you cast an evil eye on her", Daadi's reply astonished Jogi as well as Chamko. "You slut, you are showing your true colours. People like you are faithful to no one. Has that girl bribed you?" Jogi was loosing his cool.

"Say what you want. Yes, I was a slut till now but no more. I regret the days I used to sell girls to rogues like you. Champa has shown me the better side of life for which I owe a debt to her. So, listen once and for all time to come. You will leave the place right now", Daadi's speech and manners became menacing.

Jogi realised that nothing could be done on that day. He departed before daylight, hoping for a better day in the future.

6. The Mystery Unfolds

Solan was agog with rumours and gossips. The town was agonized too. Parents with young girls were worried about their safety. The most traumatized person was Lajo. Her dear friend had vanished in thin air along with her belongings. For days there was no news of Champa's whereabouts. Is she alive? The thought chilled her mind. The wait was killing. With the help of her brother Lajo took a wise step and lodged an FIR with the Kotwali regarding disappearance of Champakali. They gave vivid descriptions of the old woman and Jogi to the investigating officer. The hunt for the culprits got into full swing.

A notice appeared in the local papers,

"Search for a Kidnapped Girl,"

General public is hereby informed that this girl, whose photograph appears alongside named Champakali, better known Chamko D/O late Vaid Dayanand, R/O Preet Villa, Vikaspuri, Solan, Age 16 years, Height 5 feet, Round Face, Wheatish Complexion, Thin built, Wearing White Blouse, Blue Skirt, Long Boots, is missing since Monday. In this regard a Case FIR No. 1111/1976 dated.... U/s 363 IPC has been registered at Kotwali, Solan. Any person having any information or a clue may please inform the undersigned.

"Sd. SHO, Kotwali, Solan".

This notice and gossip became grist for the local and India media. There was a long and intensive discussion in the halls of the Public School at Dakshai. The Principal and teachers appealed to the senior boys to help in finding the girl. A group of five boys took it upon themselves to find the girl and have culprits behind bars. The boys were good at trekking. Two of them at a time would fan out and look for clues of a recent induction of new persons in the villages. Their efforts were of no avail. Then they fanned out to the forests to spot any habitation.

Champa while befriending the old woman made another move, a rather intelligent one. She convinced Daadi that they must drink boiled water to avoid stomach upset. She would burn wet wood in the 'Chulla' (stove) leading to stacks of black smoke. The idea got its reward when Praful and Raj, one day sighted that smoke coming out from a far off thicket. The slope was steep and it was raining hard, but the boys overcame all hardships. Reaching near the building, they found that the door was locked, and there was total silence around the place. Lest some body should find out their presence, Raj tried an experiment; he mewed like a cat. For a while Champa paid no attention to the cat's calls. However, their persistence made Daadi speak out, "Bitia, look out for that wretched cat and get her run away. These are nasty signals".

Champa dutifully peeped out from the window. Seeing no one she went back to her chores. Praful and Raj were overjoyed at their find. They must make sure however, that the girl they were looking for, was in there. They waited patiently, at a distance from where the window could be seen.

Some thing tugged at Chamko's heart. Every few minutes she would stand at the window, hoping for something to happen. Ultimately Praful revealed his presence. To assure the girl, he showed her the school emblem on the jacket. Chamko then knew that the investigator was a genuine fellow and she could trust him. Soon a packet landed out in the yard which Praful lapped up. It was a handkerchief, which bore her name, and in it was a 'silver trinket'. The rest was routine and easy.

The policemen swooped on the den, broke open the door and took hold of the old woman and the girl. They repatriated the belongings and the girl to her house and locked up the 'chachi'. Police investigations led them to Rudra Dev, alias 'Aardi', who confessed that he had called in a few 'goondas' and bribed them to remove her from the scene. He divulged that Jogi was the leader of that group who after kidnapping her had kept the gold ornaments, precious stones and cash for himself. Fortunately he did not molest the girl and was only persuading her to marry him. The police had the task of hounding the main culprit before taking any action. Champakali was lodged at Lajo's house to avoid recurrence of a similar attempt. 'Aardi' was put under police custody. But where was Jogi?

Soon after the revelations of the abduction episode, strange things went happening at the Dakshai School. Praful's grey flannels were missing. Raj's 'dal' was full of 'kankars' (small stones). The third boy's feet were punctured, because somebody had placed sharp pieces of glass in them. And similar assaults were made on the belongings of the remaining members of the group of 5 who had helped to track Chamko's whereabouts. The Principal set the Head-boy of the hostel, to track down the person who was creating mischief against the five-'Samaritans'.

The investigating team received their lead from the description of Jogi given by Champa and 'Aardi'. They zeroed on Sandy the head-cook, a young man of about 25 years, who showed no emotion, outwardly, while on work. Sandy would disappear from his quarters, about midnight, every day. Mostly he went to the bar and would return drunk about dawn. Once he took to the lone hutment from where Chamko was found, along with his accomplices. Little did they realise that they were being tracked. When the policemen pounced on them, one of them blurted out, "Sir that is your man, Jogi. I was not in that squad when Chamko was abducted from her house". This man's name was Naraina.

7. The Court Decides

Two murders and the abduction of Champakali were serious crimes to be tried at the Sessions Court which was held in Shimla in those days. Champa, Lajo and Praful were provided police protection and were escorted to the court in the police van. The publicity of these happenings through newspapers motivated journalists and parents of young girls to fill the court to its capacity. A wide big table on a high platform was for the Presiding Officer, (the Sessions Judge) of the proceedings. Immediately below on the floor was another table around which sat the Clerk of the Court and a typist. Leaving some space were tables for the Prosecution and Defence Lawyers. Further down were benches for citizens and the general public. Wooden frameworks were placed between the Judge's platform and his clerks while another one was set between lawyers' area and the benches for the public. On either side were slightly raised platforms, both of which were circumscribed by wooden frames. The RHS (facing the Judge) was for witnesses and the one on the LHS was for the accused.

Just as the clock struck ten, the Judge walked in. All the audience stood up in his honour, while lawyers and clerks bowed to his presence. This formality is a reminder that a judge is a learned man. He is the impartial and objective assessor, because of his deep knowledge of laws of the country, and an expert analyser of the evidence produced before him. While showing respect to the judge, everyone expresses respect towards laws of the country, because of which it is a practice, world over, to bow as the judge enters the court room. His arrival is announced by the guard, who stands behind his seat throughout the proceedings, to secure safety of the high dignitary.

The Public Prosecutor began, "Your Lordship, the State of Himachal Pradesh brings before you three culprits to be prosecuted for heinous crimes. They are:

1. Rudra Dev S/O Late Maha Dev, R/O 3/32 Krishna Gali, a medical practitioner by profession at shop

no. 41 the Raja Bazaar, Solan is (a) charged under, Indian Penal Code, IPC... of conspiracy, with Jaggi/ Sandy, Naraina and Aish Bhagwan (not traced yet) of getting killed Hakim Dayanand and his wife Kulwanti, through a third party and is also (b) charged under IPC...of conspiracy to get a minor abducted from her house, with ulterior intentions.

2. Jogi popularly called Sandy S/O Late Hari Prasad, R/O Hostel No. 3, Room No. 45, Public School Digshai, is (a) charged under IPC...for conspiracy as listed at (b) above and is charged under IPC... abducting a minor and keeping her unlawfully in a house.

3. Daadi alias Chachi, named Laila D/O Late Roshan Maharaj R/O Harvilas Gali, Kalka in aiding and abetting the other two accused in carrying out the minor's abduction and keeping her against her will in a house. She is of ill reputation and would have placed the minor girl in prostitution.

All the accused turned in "Not guilty", pleas.

Mr. Gian prasad Katju, the Sessions Judge, after listening to the prosecution and defence witnesses and the arguments of the rival counsels, wrote in his judgment:

"For once I am more than satisfied that the police have done its investigations to the full. Moreover, Naraina the conspirator turned 'approver' has provided irrevocable accounts of conspirators meetings at which the two conspiracies were hatched. His revelations match with the records of absence of Jogi from his duty at the hostel. Naraina has also provided details of the money received by conspirators and matching withdrawals of money from the accounts of Rudra Dev in the State Bank of India, Solan. But his most startling revelation is that Rudra Dev, the medico, was also responsible for the killing of Dayanand and Kalawanti. According to Naraina, the accused No. 1 could not stand the Vaid's rising popularity and increasing wealth. Mad with jealousy he got his rival eliminated through a professional killer, Aish Phalwan. I am satisfied with the identification of the spot, which I personally visited, from where the shots were fired, and the place from where the revolver was dug out. The Prosecution produced two forensic experts, from the Forensic Laboratory, Hyderabad, to prove that the weapon used to kill the parents of Champa, was the same as the one produced in the court. I record that I asked one of the experts, "Do the distance and the direction of the shot match the bullet spots on the bodies of the deceased?" "Yes, my Lord. I can say that without any hesitation", the experts corroborated turn by turn. I am satisfied by their assertion. However, I must record that the charge of conspiracy to murder and the actual murder need to be proven without a shred of doubt. Therefore the police authorities should pursue further vigorously the hunt for Phalwan. In the meantime I find charge (a) proven against Rudra Dev and all the charges proven against the accused No. 2. While the accused No. 3 did involve herself in the nefarious act of Champakali's abduction and unlawful confinement, it is a matter of conjecture that Champa would have been led to prostitution. Giving due consideration to all facts and the evidence produced before me I award the following sentences, "Rudra Dev is to undergo seven years rigorous imprisonment and a fine of Rs.10,000 or six months additional rigorous imprisonment if he fails to pay the fine.

"Jogi/Sandy is to undergo seven years rigorous imprisonment. He is fined Rs. 2000 or three months rigorous imprisonment in lieu thereof.

"Laila acquitted in view of the brave resistance she put up to save Champa from the clutches of Sandy. She risked her life. Her subsequent behaviour also deserves a reprieve.

"I commend the intelligence and bravery of Champakali. The Government of Himachal Pradesh must ensure protection to her for the next 5 years, in view of loss of her parents. "I commend the investigating officers of the police department. They should be suitably rewarded.

"Naraina is acquitted for having turned an approver and for providing crucial help to the police in unraveling the conspiracies and evidence there for". The journey back home was very enjoyable for the police and the three erstwhile hapless young persons. The audience for once felt that 'Justice was well done!'

8. Lajo's Travails

Champakali on return did not go to Preet Villa, instead felt at home at Lajo's house. The two parentless girls found solace in each other's company. Kailashnath, Lajo's brother worked for the Northern Railways and was stationed at Kalka. A Guard on goods trains, once a while his duty brought him pass through Solan, when he would say a hello to the girls, who always would prepare a wholesome meal for him. That short get-together was heavenly for all the three persons, besides a work-out on lists of articles to be replenished from Kalka. Of course the young man did spend his weekly off with them, when life was full of fun and joy.

Lajo had neglected her health when Champakali's whereabouts were unknown. Rain or shine she would go from pillar to post enquiring about her friend. On many days she missed her meals and got soaked in rain. The changing weather and the trauma of possible loss of a dear friend for ever, affected her frail physique. Ever so often she would fall ill. Chamko would become very uncomfortable with Lajo's health. Gradually the ailing lass picked up coughing and suffered from mild fever for weeks on end. Initial medication by Champakali, mostly on herbal extracts gave temporary relief only. She and Kailashnath consulted the local physician.

"She coughs and feels pain in her chest", informed Champa.

"She runs temperature all day long", Kailashnath told the doctor.

"For how long has this been going on?" asked the physician.

"For two months at the least".

"Please keep a record of her temperature and save the sputum for testing", advised the doctor.

"Did anyone in the family have 'tapedick', T.B.?" doctor's voice was heavy.

Kailashnath revealed that their grandfather had suffered from T.B. "Do you think Lajo has contracted that deadly disease?" the brother's anxiety echoed in his question.

"Its possibility cannot be ruled out". Before the doctor could say anything Lajo started crying loud and proper, "I too am destined to die".

The physician admonished her, "Don't be silly. Firstly, let me establish that you have T.B. Secondly, T.B. is completely curable". He asked for the girl's chest X-ray, and prescribed anti-allergic hydrochlorides plus expectorants to relieve her cough and fever, though temporarily. In the meantime, Lajo was asked to cover her mouth with a mask; a clean piece of cloth. She must collect her sputum in a bowl to be always kept covered. All her clothings and utensils be segregated from the rest and cleaned and disinfected thoroughly; even dried in the open when the sunshine is clear and hot.

Champa was asked to cover her mouth while conversing or treating Lajo. She must have the collection in the sputum-bowl boiled with a liter of water and disposed off daily in a covered drain which must be disinfected regularly. T.B. is a contagious disease. It can spread to others when exposed to sneezing and coughing of the affected persons, the doctor advised them. Champa noted down each and every insturction of that kind soul. Lajo was not reassured in spite of the doctor's soothing words. She took up with her friend,

"Champa be honest. Will I live?"

"You will".

"How can you be so sure?" the ailing girl persisted.

Champakali reasoned, the Government of Himachal provides elaborate funds and facilities to curb and cure this disease. Our sanitariums have the latest equipment and achieved extremely successful record of ensuring effective surveillance and follow up of cured cases to avoid their recurrence". She added "My dear every day nearly 5000 new cases of T.B. are diagnosed. Only 100 of the old and new patients die in one day. In other words, about 95% of T.B. patients can be cured, and they survive, provided DOTS is adhered to for the specified time...To assure her friend further, Champa continued, "The treatment of curing T.B. is very well proven now. This long speech from Champa and her affectionate looks put Lajo's fears at rest, at least for that evening.

The bad news surfaced when a patch was seen on the X-Ray of her chest. A gloom descended on Lajo but Champa was calm and thoughful. It was a known fact that hills' population was easy prey to this deadly disease, because of malnutrition and habitual smoking. The brave girl pursued with the local M.L.A. and sought the Civil Surgeon's help. Lajo was referred to the Sanitarium at Dharampur.

The hospital at Dharampur, about 20 kilometers downwards on the Kalka road had earned all India reputation. The Government of Himachal Pradesh ensured complete isolation of the hospital from urban areas. The best of the doctors, equipment and medicines were provided to cure patients suffering from tuberculosis of all types, particularly of lungs and bones. Research was also conducted to develop new medicinal therapies to eradicate T.B.

The doctors were very pleased to note that the girls were observing the basic precaution of using masks. They prescribed tests of Lajo's sputum, three times within a week, to confirm that Lajo was T.B. positive. However, they were highly pleased to see that the girls were observing all precautions to avoid passing on infection to each other and others who came close to them. Those three visits to Dharampur, in a week, proved time consuming besides adding financial burden. The sanitarium doctors advised treatment at the hospital, because of traces of blood in Lajo's sputum. The treatment was free (or a nominal charge) for poor patients who were placed in General Wards. The expenses for a Private Ward were estimated around ten thousand rupees. Now that was a massive amount of money. To arrange that sum appeared a big hurdle in restoring Lajo to health. Champakali tried to mortgage her parental bungalow. Kailashnath could obtain a loan of one thousand rupees from his Provident Fund. Alas the total intake could not be more than seven thousand rupees. And Lajo was taken the next day, accompanied by Champa, to the Dharampur sanitarium for admission in a General Ward. Champa decided to look after her lifelong friend in addition to the ward nurses.

The exercise turned out a horrowing and stressful experience. There was a plethora of forms to be filled in. At every window the attendants created hurdles. Champa was totally unaware of this tribe and ran into argument with every one of them. She did not know that 'a tip' moved matters faster. Since she did not pay "lubricants", Champa was stopped, by one of the women-attendants from seeing the CMO (Chief Medical Officer). "Doctor Sahib is busy in a meeting. Thereafter it will be his evening pooja time", the attendant said. Lajo was dead tired because of the day's ordeal. Champa apprehended that Lajo would not make to the CMO till the closing time, in spite of holding the complete pile of papers. This meant another visit which annoyed the girls. She shouted, "You are 'haramkhor' (pontificating on others money)". Her pink face was crimson-red and the slim body was vibrating outrageously. The 'hangama' brought into the corridor, a number of hospital employees, one of whom was Pujari Patel, a doctor who had joined the sanitarium hardly six months earlier.

"What is the matter? Why are you shouting?" he asked Champa. "I am not shouting for nothing. The woman does not let us in. We are struggling for the second day running to get admission into a general ward. Is it because we are poor that we are treated with scant regard", Champa reeled out her fury, loud and proper.

Patel took the attendant to task, ordered her to let the duo in first time on the next morning. Poojari was impressed with the girl's guts, and by her transparent and unabashed behaviour. He promised Champa of his help in getting Lajo admitted and ensure fullest attention by all concerned. Champa thanked him not superficially, but because her heart dictated so.

The following day all formalities were as smooth as butter. The CMO assured them of full recovery if the medicinal regime, DOTS (Directly Observed Treatment Short course) was observed faithfully. Pujari Patel took personal care of the duo; for them he got every facility that the hospital offered.

"It seems you love your friend immensely, "Pujari probed Champakali a few days later.

"I do. After all what are friends for, if they are not of use at times of adversity", she answered. Dr. Patel was overwhelmed by Champa's guileless reply. He could not believe that the girl from hills could be so intelligent and focused in her thoughts.

"Why do you work so hard?" he asked Champa one day.

"My friend is ill and I want her up and enjoying life once again", answered Chamko.

"Is that all?"

"Besides I want to know more about diseases and their cures", was her reply.

"You did not go to a medical school. How can you learn so much without going to an institution?" Patel expanded. But his intention was to gauge the intensity of her resolve.

"Will you teach me, doctor?" Chamko's query intrigued him. But in the few days that he had seen the lass's devotion towards Lajo, it had struck a chord in his heart.

"Of course I will", came out of his mouth without an effort. "Will you be your friend's DOTS supervisor?" he asked

"I will. What does that involve? Champa enquired.

"Don't be impatient, Chamko, let us go for a cup of tea". Chamko was surprised at Poojari's audacious offer, which however, she accepted with an undefined satisfaction.

9. Champakali's Initiation

Lajo was admitted into a ladies ward which was divided into enclosures of 6-8 beds each. The ward had wash and toilet closets besides rooms for the doctor and nurses, and medical supplies and house-keeping materials. The wards were cleaned twice daily with disinfectants. Foul air was exhausted and filtered air was let in, round the clock.

Lajo was diagnosed Category I patient. She was asked to follow DOTS for 6 months out of which it would be advisable to stay at the hospital for at lease a month. This treatment will make Lajo harmless to others. The rest of the treatment can be continued at home. "Mark it Champa, no laxness or interruption in the medication regime is acceptable. Otherwise a relapse of the disease is possible". Poojari cautioned Champakali.

Lajo was given 4 types of tablets; the pouches were labeled H,R,Z and E. The frequency and dosage were prescribed. Lajo's diet was carefully devised. Pasteurized milk, in sufficient quantity, twice daily was a must. Leafy vegetables and lentils, boiled and cooked in light oil were provided at lunch and dinner time, In between some fruit was given. All the ingredients were grown in the fields of the sanitarium and the pasteurized milk was delivered daily by Keventers of Tara Devi, at 5 in the morning. Their personal and bed spreads were sent to a central wash-room for proper treatment.

Before Dr. Patel left, Champakali asked, "What are Category II and Category III patients?" The doctor replied, "I am in a hurry, madam. Suffice it to say for the present that category II are 'Relapse' cases and are 'Serious'. They require more intensive medication; more medicines and more frequently". Without waiting for another question he walked out.

Champakali became a darling of the hospital administratrion. She took charge of 8 patients in the cubicle, as a DOTS supervisor, for the time the friends were at that sanitarium. She helped the ward nurses in their paperwork. At times she would saunter to children's ward and play games with them.

When Dr. Patel came on his round, Champa asked, "Can I ask one or two questions?"

"Why not, go ahead".

"Why do you give so many types of medicines?"

"Research has shown that the T.B. bacteria develop resistance to one or two medicines. Intense dosage of some of them, kill the germs in the patient to the extent that she/he cannot pass on the disease to others", explained Dr. Patel.

"Do all patients receive similar treatment and dosages?" Champakali was inquisitive. "No, that depends on patients' reaction to medication and the seriousness of the disease. There are some side effects of these medicines e.g. nausea, headache etc. In some cases the patients are allergic to a particular drug. Changes are made to suit patients of different categories", the doctor amplified.

"And you once talked of Category III disease. What is it?" Champa intervened. Pujari continued "Don't be impatient. I was talking of category II and I patients who are given still more types of medicines. Category III cases are either sputum negative or extra-pulmonary (other than lungs). I won't tell you any more otherwise you will replace me in this hospital", Dr. Patel laughed loudly and beckoned Lajo and Champakali towards the Pathology Department.

The doctor introduced them to the staff, one of whom showed them the samples of sputum of various kinds. The girls were astonished to see the bacteria, called '*Mycobacterium tuberculosis*'. The deadly creatures do damage to lungs and other organs similar to what white ants do to woods.

Every morning Champakali travelled from Solan to Dharampur to attend on her friend, lend a helping hand to nurses in the general ward and spend an hour or two with the doctors. All the thirty days that Lajo stayed at the sanitarium, Champa assiduously learnt the causes, treatment and preventive measures of Tuberculosis. Every little detail, of the day's happenings was put down in a diary. The two girls became popular with the patients and medical personnel. While leaving the sanitarium Champakali said, "Dr. Patel, will you set up a clinic at Solan. I can hand over my father's shop to you and I want to work for you". Dr. Poojari Patel was more than happy! The 'clinic' facilities could benefit large numbers. The invitation could serve his personal aim too. It opened the avenues of visiting Champakali.

10 They All Marry

When Chamko and Lajo left the sanitarium for Solan, Dr. Patel walked upto the main gate, to see them off. Will he meet Chamko again! But he was enthused when she looked back and waived to him. It was encouraging. The following Sunday he landed at their house unannounced.

"Hai, how are you Lajo?" Lajo knew who he had come for. Champa was out shopping and the restlessness on the visitor's face was showing.

"What can I offer you? Chamki may take some time to return", the reply was a matter of etiquette, but Lajo's intention was to tease him.

"Do not take any trouble, you are still weak. Let us first talk about you. How often are you taking your medicines?" Poojari took a detour. He must be a doctor before anything else. He must employ the time, until Chamko's return, usefully to check up Lajo's progress since her discharge from the sanitarium. It meant saving a visit of the girls to the sanitarium, involving money and time. Secondly he looked up daily records which he had asked Champakali to maintain. Fortunately Lajo showed all-round improvement. When he went to keep back those records, he saw a photograph.

"Whose photo is that Lajo?" Poojari pointed to a picture of a young girl with two groomed hair ponies. Lajo wanted to play a prank but stopped short of it, "Oh, how cutely she smiles, doctor?" she asked.

"She does", the reply was very sincere.

"That is Chamko, when she was twelve. Do you like the photograph?" she was being mischievous.

Now Chamko was slim and tall, her face long which carried a sharp nose, green cat-like penetrating eyes. Her complexion was pink spread over creamy skin centuries of cool hill air moist with pine fragrance had produced. She had a huge mass of jet black hair woven into two thick pony tails, touching her bum at the back. It was her voice which seduced one first, extremely arrogant but totally honest. Clear as the sound of a temple-bell, she never uttered words which were double-speak or veiled her intentions. All in all she was getting to be a handsome woman.

Poojari hesitated to utter a word. His body-language and his eyes betrayed him. How embarrassing are those moments, when your heart says something but words fail to come out!

He only said, "Will Champa be gone for long?"

And just that moment Chamko walked in. "Your doctor is missing you, darling", Lajo put in, throwing the obvious hint from the corner of her eye.

"Have you been here for long? I am sorry I didn't mean to keep you waiting. Have I faithfully followed your instructions? How do you find Lajo's progress?" Champa reeled off to show her faithful adherence to the healer's instructions. She was flustered and failed to register Lajo's indirect implication of the lovesick doctor.

Dr. Poojari laughed and said, "Relax Champa, you are doing excellently. How can I find fault with you? Rather I should learn a thing or two from you".

Lajo intervened, "While the two of you are learning from each other, I shall go in and make tea for you two", and she got up to proceed towards the kitchen.

The doctor was on cloud seven and interjected, "Not at all Lajo, you stay where you are. Today let me show you my hand at making tea. Champa, please come over and tell me where your pots and pans are". Lajo tittered and Champa walked along the guest rather shy and nonplussed.

Lajo made her exit saying, "Let me see why the dog is so quiet today?"

Inside the kitchen neither talked to the other. But wafts of air, blowing from the window, touched their chords. Mute melodies, withing their hearts, made them swoon. They realised that they were getting nearer but could not give a voice to their feelings.

To monitor Lajo's progress, Dr. Poojari made more than a few visits, in the following weeks. After examining Lajo, the two would saunter into lonely hill tracks. Lajo improved gradually and so did the understanding between Dr. Poojari Patel and Champakali. But the two were too shy to utter the right words. To everyone's surprise a middle aged woman, elegantly dressed, knocked at the door one afternoon, "Is this Champakali's house?" she asked.

Champa opened the door, and uttered hesitatingly, "Yes 'Mata Ji'. I am Champa". While she bowed, Lajo and the guest exchanged smiles.

"God bless you", came out voluntarily.

Kailashnath dropped in. Lajo and he got busy in looking after the guest. Champa was getting nowhere when Dr. Poojari walked in, "Mother, you here?" His voice was no more than a whisper. His eyes popped wide open, as if he had been struck with lightning.

Gradually the puzzle was unlocked. Lajo had arranged the whole episode to put a seal on the relationship between her friend and the dotting-totting friendly doctor. The lady had been invited from Ahmedabad to see and approve her son's would-be wife. The gracious lady was more than happy and approved of their wedding which was duly celebrated on Diwali Day. Kailashnath was only too happy to act the elder brother to Chamko and perform the religious rituals.

Preet Villa bloomed into an abode of happiness where Champakali lived with Poojari. Lajo found a capable groom, a teacher. Kailashnath, posted at Kalka railway station, helped Champa in obtaining medicines from firms in Delhi.

11. The Future is Bright

Within a year of their wedding, Chamko delivered a baby girl. "Chamko's Chamki", Poojari announced the girl's name proudly. The parents became too conscious about her upbringing. Any and every research on child upbringing was studied and took in the useful tips. Dr. Patel said one day, "Champa, research shows that three quarters of the human brain develops after birth. Development of the brain has a direct relationship with the child's outside environment".

"How about opening a good play-school to help developing children's brain? Chamki will benefit from the company of other children. Lajo and her spouse can be sent for special training in Montessori and related teaching methodologies". Poojari and Lajo were taken aback at the speedy reaction and proposals from Champakali. The 'project school' was on.

By the time Chamki was three, Preet Villa was converted into a pre-nursery school, 'Step-by-Step Angels', for children between 3-5 years. The interiors were done up in bright colours. On the walls were paintings of trees, animals, cars, aircrafts etc. In play rooms there was abundance of toys. Utmost stress was placed on hygienic aspects of the premises and the children. Ever so often the premises were fumigated and drains carried live fish to devour mosquitoes.

Champakali proudly explains to the parents of the new students, "Children's energy is channelized through painting, playing on musical instruments, singing and dancing. Specialised computer programmes used to teach phonetics, numbers shapes and colours. The tiny tots have a couple of deer and dogs, of a few selected pedigrees, to play with in the park which surrounds the school building. Vegetables are grown in small quantities so that the little ones can recognise potatoes, peas, cauliflowers, reddish and carrots. Apples, plums and pears' trees are also raised. This part of the school curriculum is accomplished with help from parents of the wards. The parents also gather on every second Sunday to take the children on rides to the railway station, police station, post office and the market places. Most of the school kids get admission into the Dakshai's Public School or well known schools at Shimla and even Delhi, merely because of the reputation of 'Step-by-Step Angels', bright prodigies".

12. The Epilogue

Poojari and Champakali have come a long way. A clinic advocating naturopathy and treatment with locally available herbal medicines is run by Champakali. People come there from far and wide. Kailashnath and his wife help her at the clinic. The poor belonging to Solan receive free treatment. Poojari continues to work at the Dharampur sanitarium. Such of the patients who require hospitalization are looked after by him. No graft and no harassment. 100 per cent medical attention is assured to Poojari's patients.

Time has come to reveal a secret. My name is Praful, the boy who along with Raj rescued Champakali. I am the son of a retired I.A.S. Officer. 40 years ago, he was posted as S.D.M. of Solan. My schooling was initiated at the residential Public School at Dakshai. From that day onward I followed that 'Madonna' of my dreams and would have succeeded in marrying her but for the intervention of the doctor. After finishing at the school I rented a room near Champa's house so that I could trail every moment of my beloved's life. In my free time I made portraits of her, which you can see if you happen to visit Solan. Because of my devotion I preserved every detail of her life which I have described, so that you too can admire the guts and intelligence of an ordinary girl who is making extraordinary contribution in every facet of her life. Chamki looks like her mother and is as bright as Chamko would have been. I only hope she does not face bad days like her mother. Instead, she adds to the traditions of service of her family; Dayanand, Champakali, Poojari Patel and their associates Lajo and Kailashnath.

As for myself I live alone till this day. She was the girl for me and none else ever replaced her in my dreams and thoughts! ❑❑

Note: (a) The Guppy and Gambusia which are playthings in house-hold acquariums can be effective in controlling malaria and water-borne diseases. NDMC has successfully used the fishes in a drain near the Prime Minister's house, and in fountains ad ponds. Civic authorities are introducing them in wells, tanks, lakes and paddy fields instead of DDT and chemical sprays.

(b) The medical terms and medication may Not please be used for self-medication or treating a T.B. patient.

The Runaways

On a dark, rainy and muggy evening the bell rang. On opening the door Narayni was surprised to see Pratibha her two daughters and her sister Preeti along with the latter's son Ashish. Twenty years ago the women had left them and they now appeared out of thin air, dripping wet yet beaming. Narayni hugged the women, patted affectionately the young ones and treated them to 'Nashta' as per custom of the house. Narayni and the women got busy in narrating the happenings to each and every one since their departure and till reappearance on that day. Harish, Narayni's husband, also landed about the same time. He was amazed to see the brood. Saying a symbolic 'Namaste', he rushed to freshen up. His mind flashed back while he was taking his bath.

He recalled that soon after his arrival in Delhi Narayni had delivered twins. She, soon after the delivery, developed urinary infection, leaving the infants without their mother's milk. They were in dire need of help-hands. For him the two women, whom the security guard ushered in, were god sent. The guard happened to be their neighbour in the cluster of shanties. Pratibha and Preeti claimed to be sisters, though in ages and appearance they were not alike at all. They stated their ages 40 years and 25 years respectively; the age difference seemed odd. The older one was extremely frail and fair but the less aged, the other one was stout and fulsome and she hobbled (Later on it became known that she had Jaipur Foot on her left leg). She was of a darker complexion too. The older stated to have two girls who were left in the juggie. The younger one carried a three month old boy, whom she carried on her bosom.

"Sir, we need work desperately" beseeched the older of the two. "My name is Pratibha and she is Preeti, my sister. We will do anything and everything you want us to do. I learn Mem-Sahib is ill. Preeti will take care of your babies; even suckle them till Mem-Sahib recovers".

"But who stands guarantee for you?" asked Harish.

"Sahib we lived in 'Shaktishalini' free home till a few days back. You can verify our antecedents with them", answered Pratibha.

"You better bring a letter of recommendation from that NGO", Harish demanded.

"But Sir give us the job right now because our children are terribly hungry", begged Pratibha with folded hands. "I promise to fetch the letter before you go to office tomorrow" she offered.

By a coincidence the twins were screaming at the top of their voices, throwing a hint not to delay the engagement of maids any more. Common needs and their respective interest of survival converged, overruling any lurking doubts about their antecedents and previous experience. The formalities could wait. Harish was relieved to hire them because there was no bargaining on salaries and other niceties. Peace prevailed that night in the bureaucrat's house. Pratibha took on responsibilities of cleaning, washing clothes and cooking. Preeti remained busy caring for the darlings, from suckling to washing their nappies and much more.

Pratibha brought the letter from the Head of Shaktishalini as she had promised. It said that their sincerity, hard working habits and total devotion to allotted duties earned them high appreciation at that women's help home. Later on these very attributes endeared them to one and all, including Narayni's neighbours. Above all their darlings, Mukti and Mukesh, grew very fond of Preeti. The maids were given, some days later, quarters to live in.

Narayni was astonished to find one day Pratibha saying Namaaz in her quarters. A Muslim in the household! Fatima explained, "Madam my name was changed at "Shaktishalini" wherefrom I came to you. People in Delhi, I am told give jobs more easily to Hindu or Christian maids. I shall narrate my true story to you whenever you have spare time". Narayani, though, belonged to an orthodox Hindu family; the issue of two different religions living under the same roof never came up during her upbringing. 'Trust and sincerity only should matter', she thought to herself. Narayni and Harish pondered over this revelation for a while. They decided to close the chapter once for all. Fatima remained Pratibha, that time onward, for one and all. Fatima continued her 'namaz' and all her religious rituals with Narayni with her husband's support.

Gradually the women opened up to Harish's wife. Narayni kept her husband up-dated every night. It came out that Pratibha and Preeti are not born of same parents. They are just soul-sisters (Moonh Boli Bahenain). Their past lives were unhappy which is not uncommon with women in our country.

Pratibha was born in the crowded centre of Hyderabad and baptized as Fatima. Her father, a carpenter earned hardly enough to support five siblings, his wife and old parents. Sweetie, the nicknamed Fatima, was the youngest of three brothers and one sister besides her. She brought luck to her father who made a break with a builder in Kuwait. Liberal money came regularly from Mian Faiz thereafter. The family moved to a rented, bigger, house. They lived comfortably, the boys and girls began going to schools. Fatima was not allowed to go beyond her middle school, the highest level of education that girls of her sect and social standing were allowed to attain. Besides, she became proficient in cooking, and dress making especially ladies blouses, which hugged exquisitely her customers' curvaceous bodies. There was no problem in finding a suitable match for her, as the brothers and father were earning handsome fortunes and had also acquired a house of their own. Their social standing stood high. Her soul-mate, Nawaz Sharif, young and handsome was a trained electrician. The future looked favourable for the newly married.

To her in-laws' and parents' delight she got into family-way very soon after living with her husband. A joy-making function to celebrate the impending arrival of a child (hopefully a son) was arranged. Sharif, drinking fish-like in that party, got the taste of free booze of his father-in-law's gifts from Kuwait. However the evening chimes sounded bells of the doom-days (unknown to them) arrival too. Thereafter, the son-in-law expected those and many more goodies regularly and very soon started demanding liquor parcels as a matter of right. His skill rotted and earnings dried up. Fatima's husband became over-lordly and forced her to fetch money too from her brothers whenever he desired a good evening out with his mates. Sweetie's family did not want her to suffer at all, though the helpless wife felt humiliated to ask monetary help from her mother and brothers, time and again. "I was living in a hell", said Fatima rolling out torrents of tears, explained to Narayani.

"Did Nawaz molest you, I mean hit you, when he asked for his price of being your man?" Narayni asked of the maid.

"Nako Huzoor. I was never attacked bodily. He did not use his hands, a stick or hurt me physically", replied the maid. She went on, "He would threaten to harm my brothers. Abused me in foul expletives and kept his harangues going all night long keeping me awake and hungry".

"Madam, I got a girl in my first delivery which disappointed my in-laws, and even myself. It became another peg for Sharif to post his complaints upon. For the sake of keeping our social standing, a few usual celebrations were arranged. The merry making by my husband, because of free gifts from my parents, gave me respite for a while from his taunts and bad mouthing. My baby was named Sheereen, hoping for the sweeter days ahead", Fatima paused.

"And thereafter?" the mistress asked

"I conceived again. Since this time I became pregnant too soon after the birth of the first child, my body failed to stand upto the stress, especially in view of our domestic night long strives, day in and day out. My blood pressure soared which resulted in an unhealthy girl child, besides a weakened physique of mine. It meant neglecting needs of the newly born", explained the house help.

To cut the long story short, Fatima became more dependent on her parent's family, who were always out to help her. She again conceived and, unluckily for her, failed to get a male heir for the her husband. Her travails grew in numbers and intensity. Off and on she would go to her mother's house, avoiding her husband's harassment. But he never let her stay there long, insisting that her frequent visits to her parents lowered him in the eyes of his neighbours and society. Fatima got used to an unsettled life when an enexpected tragedy struck. In spite of the constant medical attention given to the second girl, the sickly child succumbed to her congenital shortcomings. Fatima was shattered.

But her cold blooded mate relentlessly asked for his 'Hafta (weekly gratification)'. Fatima's mother came to her support always, but the harassed woman's mind was gathering a storm.

One evening, a diktat from Sharif came like a stroke of lightning, "I need 500 rupees this week". He had lost 200 bucks on betting at the races. When Fatima remonstrated, the shafts of expletives were rained on her. Suddenly her eldest daughter, Sheereen shrieked, "Nahin Baba, Mat Marna Maa Ko, (Father please don't hit my mother)". Fatima, who till then was looking at the floor was shaken to see the raised hand of her man, ready to slap her. The woman could take no more. She suddenly turned diplomatic and said, "Sahi Ho, (O.K.) I am going to my mother for the last time and will be back in two days with the money". She gathered a few belongings and her two girls reaching her mother's house rather late at night. No questions were asked. That household guessed the reason for the untimely visit.

Fatima, because of the gathering steam within, was considering of other options. 'Her kind and considerate

---

Note: The amounts in rupees, on this and other pages, relate to prices in 1990s.

kin will respond to her husband's calls to save her from abuses and insults, perhaps body-blows too in the future. But why should she spend the gifted money on his inconsiderate husband's booze and bets? Why should she not spend the same money on her daughters and her own sustenance? And then another thought occurred to her. 'If she has to beg from her mother and brothers for all times, then she can also beg at a Dargah if not on road side'. The steam within Fatima blew the lid off! She took courage and decided to break loose for ever from her relatives and friends. Collecting 500 rupees in the evening she took leave from her mother and brothers' families, holding back her swelled up tears. The fugitives went to Hyderabad railway station and boarded the Janta Express to Delhi. She had heard of Nizamm-ud-Din Dargah there. From then on the Dargah was her restitution! "Since leaving home I have never cried again, memsahib", said Fatima proudly. Narayni was astonished at the giant step taken by the lone and meek woman with two kids on that evening. And the self confidence on top of it all!

The family of three reached in Nizam-ud-Din Dargah without a problem. Fatima was alloted a place for her family in the dormitory for the destitute. She was entitled to free accommodation and food for odd jobs at the Lord's house. But the woman's self-esteem bobbed up, "Why should I live on charity? Within a few weeks she was enabled to join an NGO. "Shaktishalini" (The House of Energy) which helped in training women of poor homes to learn a few skills, get employment and earn sufficient money to sustain themselves.

Fatima continued her narrative. "The first act that I did was to remove my 'Burkha' and move around freely within the premises. There were many women of my religion there. Exchanges of our experiences of cruelty and maltreatment, helped remove mental tension. In due course the depression and the feeling of helplessness also vanished. Hopes swarmed in gradually and my self-confidence increased day by day. I met Preeti at Shaktishalini of whom I shall tell you later".

"Did you ever think of your mother and brothers?" asked Narayni. "They must be worried about you, Fatima", the mistress explained "Ji Maalik. I wrote home to my mother informing her of my safe existence at the "Shaktishalini. There was a frantic telephone call to return. A police case, of abduction and keeping me at a secret location, had been filed against my mother and brothers by Nawaz Sharif. I didn't panic. Instead, I had a letter written by the NGO-In-Charge to the effect that I was residing there of my free will. The high-tone letter had the desired effect. The police dropped all cases against my family members.

Harish and Narayni were impressed with the growing adroitness of the maid. "Living within a shell breeds laziness of body and mind beneath the aura of ineffectiveness. Breaking barriers is the only way to survive in this hard world, Memsahib" said Fatima one afternoon.

There was little left of Fatima's narrative. After overthrowing her veil, she became Pratibha, the name which was chosen for her by the inmates of the NGO home. Very soon she got the job of cleaning an office, nearby, in the mornings and after office hours. She earned remuneration to be easy about her living expenses and even enough to have her older girl admitted in a municipality run school. Shaktishalini management, having completed their task, and responsibility, of uplifting the woman to live by her own efforts, asked her to leave the free home and look for her own place. Narayni stopped Pratibha at this point to know of her bonds with Preeti. "Maalik, Preeti lived in a village, a few kilometers off the town of Bhiwani in Haryana. Sturdily built and in her youthful prime, she became the favourite of a soldier. She had already done her pre-graduation, when a army man forced the girl and her parents to marry her to him. But the 'Services duties' hardly left them together for more than a few months at a time. In his absence the girl was wooed by her 'Dever' the soldier's younger brother. This was not acceptable to Preeti. Fortunately she conceived when her husband came for a brief stay. But the inevitable happened. Her husband was killed, by Nagas, somewhere in the north-east. Thereafter, the pressure from her 'Dever' increased. Her in-laws, even the village Panchyat, considered the proposed relationship constitutional (according to local tradition). The pitch for her new wedding reached obnoxious limits for her. One evening she was beaten up so badly that her leg was fractured. Giving no care to her bleeding leg, the following evening, drenched in falling rain, she boarded a train to Delhi. She was apprehended by the police at Delhi railway station and passed on to Nari Niketan by orders of a court".

"Why did she not go to her parents?" asked Narayni.

"Her parents died while she was an infant and was raised by uncles and aunties. After the girl's marriage, none of them came forward to provide her their shelter or support", explained Pratibha. "To cut the story short, the Nari Niketan handed her over to Shaktishalini where she was resided in the room I was staying. Because of lack of care, her injury became infectious and the leg had to be partially amputated. Hearts have no reasons madam. I considered her my ward from the day she reached my room. Moreover, she looked after my girls when I was away to my employer. We became, 'Moon Boli Behens'. Shaktishalini management helped her to get the Jaipur foot fitted. In due course she delivered a boy. Since we were not entitled to live longer in Shaktishalini we decided to look for two jobs in the same house. And that is how we reached your home, Maalik".

Pratibha and Preeti left Harish's household 5 years later, when their twins were handed over to a governess. Moreover the ladies had made enough money to buy a juggie in a nearby cluster. Preeti opened a beauty parlour in the hut. There were celebrations in the slum very frequently. Pratibha provided meals for guests and Preeti groomed the bride and local girls. Together they did roaring business. The handsome income helped them raise the girls and the boy in good schools and colleges.

"What have your girls done Pratibha?" asked Harish as, by then, he had joined the gathering. "Sahib, Sheereen has graduated in Home Science from the Lady Irwin College. She is a specialised dietician and recently got a job at Navjeevan hospital". Pratibha's voice resonated with a sense of pride in her daughter's achievement.

"And Azeeza"?

She is at the National Fashion Institute. Hopefully she shall finish her course with distinction and relieve me of all worries.

Now was Preeti's turn. Her boy Ashish was brilliant in Manthematics. He was studying Mechanical Engineering at the Delhi College of Engineering, "What are you planning to do young man?" asked Harish. Preeti looked at her son to answer.

The boy said, "Sir I am in a team of 12 boys who have designed a solar car and built a pro-type too.

We are going to display it at a rally of solar cars in Washington, where 30 more teams are competing. I suppose we will succeed in selling our car to a major automobile manufacturer".

"Son, you will win", Harish said enthusiastically.

"Why do you say so, Sir?"

"Young man 'Where there is a Will there is a Way'. It is exactly what your mothers and you have exhibited; courage, determination, passion and the resolve to succeed always".

"Thank you, sir".

After that friendly phase in their dialogues came the real purpose of the guests visit. Pratibha handed over a smart invitation card to Narayni, "Huzoor ko Sheereen Kee Shadi per Aana Zaroor", tears of affection came out.

Harish was touched to the core by the affectionate tone of his erstwhile maid. "We will definitely come to the wedding, Pratibha".

"Allah, Aap Ko Barkat Bakshe".

God fearing woman's blessings will materialize, mused Narayni! ❑❑

Our Prime Minister

She met me at Gaylord, a well-known restaurant in Connaught Place at Delhi where I had invited her for dinner, the day after we were engaged. Till then, she had been answering questions about herself from me and my parents. Therefore, that day there was no inhibition, which was quite evident from her free talk and the questions that were asked.

"Is Bhopal a big city?" seemed a natural one, as I had been appointed a senior manager in Bharat Heavy Electricals (BHEL) after seven years' stay in the United Kingdom.

The year was 1960, BHEL's activities had just begun. Being away on the outskirts of the old city of Bhopal, my answer was "The city is of good size, but not as big as Delhi. We will stay in the colony built for our company's employees. In due course, there will be all amenities and facilities".

"Do you get Coca Cola there?"

This certainly was a bouncer and least expected by me. During the six months that I had been in India, this drink had no place in my lifestyle. On one or two occasions, when I happened to be in Delhi or Bombay, I had tasted this newly introduced American wonder. Bhopal was too small a place, according to Coca Cola's marketing strategy.

"No, Coca Cola is not available there. But some other cold drinks ought to be available. Anyway, I don't like its taste".

This revelation was a faux pas. The giggling girl was visibly disappointed; Bhopal came down in her estimation. Noticing this down slide, I ventured to buoy her up.

"The company has given me a big bungalow with a lawn in front, where you can grow flowers. In the backyard we can have vegetables. I have already planted a nimboo tree-seedless variety".

"I love flowers. Do you know, I can get up at 4.00 in the morning and tend my little ones". The vivacious tone in her voice pleased me but her getting up at 4.00 a.m. from a warm bed unnerved me.

"No, no, you don't need to do that. Our company mali can look after everything. You can be taking care of the house".

"Don't worry, darling, I will look after both; outside as well as inside. Incidentally, who cooks for you?

She had addressed me "darling" for the first time so I too felt chivalrous and without a safety guard showed up my prowess, gained over seven years independent living in flats in England. "I cook my own – vegetarian or non-vegetarian dishes and also sweet dishes. Tell me whatever you like – kheer, pudding and trifle. You will like triffle and..."

I was in full flow but she interjected, "I don't know cooking. Are you annoyed?" "Ah no, not at all. I will help you".

"There never was a chance to go to the kitchen. We always have four or five servants. One of them,

Lakshmi, exclusively attends to me. How many servants do you have?"

"None".

"None?" She was amazed! I explained "In England, I learnt to do all housekeeping. So I brought a vacuum cleaner, a long-handled broom and a mop with changeable swabs. I can do everything in fifteen to twenty minutes. No problem whatsoever". The do-all personality of mine played a damper on her expectations of a blissful married life. Being ten years older than her I knew how to deal with the gloomy situation.

"Come on let us go to a movie. There is a good one on "Around the World in Eighty Days" with David Niven".

This idea of mine proved a hit. The fantasy, adventure and David Niven's deadpan humour brought out peels of laughter from her. Thank God the day ended happily for both of us. Since that day I vowed to keep my Dolly Darling bubbly and joyful. There was a price for it though. I had to give up my English habits of self-reliance in cooking and housekeeping. From the day she entered into our bungalow at Bhopal, after a two-week long honeymoon in Kashmir, our first servant, Dharma, also joined us.

Nearly three years later, an emergency call from Dharma's (our servant) mother entailing his immediate departure for his hometown, left us helpless. The canteen manager came to our rescue. A twelve-year old Nepali boy, Lal Bahadur was the new servant.

This fellow hardly over four feet tall, cherry red faced with sparkling eyes, enticed us from day one. He could neither cook nor clean and on the slightest opportunity ran out after barking dogs or fluttering butterflies. Many a time, I had to dig him out from one of our neighbours' houses or the colony park, well over a kilometer away from our place. He would be showing off on the swing, making it ride higher to its limit. Yet my darling wife adored him.

"I am teaching him household chores one by one. He can't be perfect in one day. What is wrong if he sneaks away, after all he is a small boy? He is so handsome. Now don't you reuke him. He will leave us".

Many management skills, learnt so diligently in schools of Business Management and practiced so successfully in my office, failed miserably whenever I faced this little threat. My vow to keep peace and joy within our four walls had to face many more hardships.

"Where is Bahadur today?" I had to ask one evening when I didn't find him on returning from my office.

"Bahadur is upset with us and has gone to his quarters. His grouse is:

"Mem Saab, Aaap Saab ko egg or toast breakfast ko daiti hain. Aur mujhe raat ki roti aur chai. Yeh mujhe pasand nahin".

"So what do you propose now?" I asked my wife. "I think we should give him bread slices instead of left-over roti. Imagine if he falls sick because of indigestion". Although he had never had indigestion till then, the possibility could not be ruled out.

"Suppose he asks you for an egg and butter for his slices?" I questioned. "Now, don't you give him ideas", she told me off and continued, "I know how to deal with him".

Realizing my handicap, I left my wife and Bahadur to their peculiar kinship. I was surprised that our Bahadur agreed to bread without butter or egg, but on the condition that he would have slices toasted in our pop-up toaster. Many months passed without a mishap, one of which I always apprehended. And it did happen!

Saturday was a half-working day. I landed back from my office a little before lunch. Bahadur opened the door to me.

"Mem Saab Gupta Mem Saab ke ghar gaya. Aap ke liya botal laun?"

Bahadur's offer of a botal, cold drink from the refrigerator was welcome because it was quite hot outside and I was thirsty. "Yes, Bahadur, thanda botal le aao". Overjoyed the little fellow ran and suddenly there was a deafening explosion, Bahadur lay on the floor, blood flowing out from the deep gashes in his legs. I was terrified at the gory sight and his loud shrieks. Just then, my wife entered. "What's happened?"

Bahadur had opened the fridge with a jerk, letting slip the soda-bottle from his hand. On falling, the gas within it caused the explosion and shattered the glass bottle. The flying pieces of glass cut deep into his legs. Without waiting, we rushed him to the hospital, from where he was discharged after three weeks. For three more weeks we served him at the house until he could hobble about.

Came the fateful Thursday of 1964. We had gone to our offices and came the sad news of the death of Jawahar Lal Nehru. A sense of mourning went through all around. I along with some colleagues collected in our sitting room. For a while, we recalled the anecdotes of Jawahar Lal Nehru's services to the Indian Nation and to the freedom of many countries from colonial rulers. Bahadur was listening to our narrations while serving water or tea to the guests. He asked me, when all of them had gone,

"Saab, Jawahar Lal kaun thaa?"

"Hamara Prime Minister. Tum samjho woh desh ka rajah thaa."

"Us ko kya hua, jo aap sub officer ghar jaldi aa gai?"

"Bahadur, us rajah ka dehant ho gaya. Woh bhaut achha rajah thaa".

"To, ab koyi naya rajah banega?

I was not then in a mood to listen to his pitter-patter and asked him to leave me alone.

A few days later, Lal Bahadur Shastri became Prime Minister of India. Bahadur came over to me, with the newspaper carrying his photograph.

"Saab, yeh kaun hai?"

"Hamara naya rajah".

"Is ka naam kaya hai?"

"Lal Bahadur Shastri". His face fell and I asked him "Kayun Kaya hua?"

"Saab, naam to mera be Lal Bahadur hai. Per kismat apna apna. Woh rajah hai, aur main naukar".

I was dumbfounded. Did he really mean to be our Prime Minister! ❑❑

Floppy

One more transfer. This time from Delhi to Calcutta. Three years' stay in Delhi, saw our house charmingly dressed up with furniture and furnishings. And now to dismantle, pack, and load them and then the reverse operations at Calcutta. I was full of resentment, thinking that his Lordship (my husband) had desired all things done up by the next evening. The door bell rang and I grudingly opened the door.

Bubble stood there with a few days old pup in his hands. Spotted black and white, silky fur, the tiny creature made me soft.

"It is lovely, where did you get it from?"

"Mom, it belongs to Auntie of B-70X. It is worth Rs. 700". He felt encouraged by my first response and yet tried to impress me by the pup's high worth.

"Yes, the fellow is charming" and I took him in my arms to care him. "Put him in your lap and feel his soft and smooth skin, Maa" and Bubble ran his small palms over his body.

I forgot about my chores and offered biscuits to the puppy. He lapped them up in no time and his greedy eyes were still pinned on the packet of biscuits in my hands when I lovingly rebuked "Get along little fellow. Enough is enough". Handing over the pup to Bubble I added "Now you take him back to his home. Don't waste time any more. Get your elder brother Vicky, back here promptly. Both of you put your belongings together. I have no time for your tasks".

Bubble was crestfallen, still he kissed the pup and taking him away from me muttered "Come brother, Mom won't let me play with you". He ran away to B-Block.

Half an hour later the brothers came back home. The two got into the act of collecting and arranging their wares. There was an unusual amity between the brothers on that day. In between I could hear their whispers.

"What is the matter you fellows" I called from the adjoining room as I suspected of a conspiracy, between the two brothers to guile their mother. It is ironic that the two are always at loggerheads except when they want to extract a favour from me. Suddenly Bubble came from behind and kissed me "Oh, my sweet Mummy". "Come on son, what is this buttering for?".

"Floppy is handsome, Maa, no?"

"What Floppy?"

"The fellow I brought this morning. He is called Floppy".

"It is a strange name". I was a little sarcastic.

"No Mummy, he is rightly named. He cannot keep his balance. Since he tumbles about helpless, Auntie named him Floppy".

"He is not a patch on Masha" I retorted. And just then the string of pets lives rolled before my eyes.

Masha, a Pomeranian, was egg white. Hardly seven days old he came to our house in Bangalore. We could see him in all the rooms, jumping ahead or behind

Vicky and Bubble. In the morning the fruit seller must give Masha a banana, otherwise his jaws locked at the vendor's ankles. To other visitors he was very respectful, standing on his hind legs he would join his forelegs, posturing "namaskar" to all guests. Simply adorable, we could not live without him. And then one evening Vicky carried him home dead in his arms. In the evening Masha was prancing about me as I dressed up for a farewell dinner at my husband's friend's place. Masha was unusually friendly, lapping at my feet, at my hands and all over. Sudarshan (my husband) and I got into our car and left him behind, Masha running after us. On return we saw him in deepest slumber. Yet there was no injury on his body. Next morning Masha was buried. We sobbed and vowed never to keep a pet dog!

Before Masha, we lost Blinker, Frowny and...

Just then Bubble awakened me "Dear Mummy, this Floppy is as beautiful as Masha". No, Bubble, no, Pets are not in my destiny. I lose them. Frowny, was poisoned by the Corporation staff just because he strayed out on to the road when the family was away in Bombay on a holiday".

"And then Blinker, a Lasha-Apso, with his black long and heavy locks of hair. His eyes could hardly be seen. Someone stole him. Even the efficient Bangalore Police could not trace him..."

"But Mummy, this one is so lovable. I am going to keep Him". There was defiance in Bubble's expression.

"Who is going to pay Rs. 700 for him" I argued. And this is where I got trapped. Vicky came from behind and said "Auntie asks for no money. Free, Mummy, free. Now you can have no objection".

"I have objection. He must be having some disease. Why is your Auntie so keen to get rid of him?"

"Oh, Mummy, you are full of suspicions. Auntie has a litter of four pups. She has already given away two. One she keeps and for this one she is looking for a decent home. This Floppy is the last. Please Mummy Please".

"And who is going to rear him up? I am not". I thought this would dissuade the boys.

The two came back in unison "We will. You don't have to do anything. Can we bring him now?"

"No" I did say that but my voice was so feeble that Vicky and Bubble could not have heard it. The brothers darted out at the speed of lightning and were back with that pup in just no time.

Sudarshan just laughed at my feigned resistance to the newcomer. Neither of us mattered any more. Bread, milk and an egg were mixed to make Floppy's first meal. Vicky and Bubble would not let anyone touch him that night. The two shared the same bed with Floppy in between them. They kept their bedroom locked that night and we heard no sound for a good twelve hours. And since Floppy came to our house, pre-named (baptised perhaps) by the B-Block Aunt, my husband, who had given names to all our earlier pets, lost his favourite hobby of searching a new name. Floppy was totally our two boys' prize, lock, stock and barrel!

Floppy created history the next day. Rajdhani Express to Howrah was delayed by 15 minutes. Bubble and I were in our reserved seats in the Chair Car compartment of Rajdhani.

Floppy was snugly ensconced in Bubble's lap when the ticket checking staff came.

"Madam, is this pup going with you?"

"Yes" I answered.

"Sorry, the rules do not permit a dog in passengers compartment".

"But this one is too young to be put in the reserved kennel".

"You are right, Madam. It must be unloaded".

Well, well. Bubble let hell loose on hearing this. He cried, tears and howling combined that my father, my husband and I felt completely embarrassed. The battle of wits between the boy and the Railways Authorities kept the train held up. My father's assurance to have Floppy sent by air only assuaged Bubble, who kept on crying for an hour after Floppy was detrained and Rajdhani left for Howrah.

Floppy's travel by the Indian Airlines was one of 007 exploits by my husband. He was to fly from Delhi, after about two weeks of my arrival at Calcutta. Someone advised him to put the fellow in a basket with a muzzle on his mouth. That is all. It seemed easy but the lady at the counter did not think it so. She prescribed a nice bunch of formalities. It must have been my husband's sheepish face that she relented and whispered "Sir, you do not declare it. Carry it along in the basket and I hope your pet does not whimper or cry. Once you are in the aircraft you (and the dog) are through".

Well, for once Floppy behaved. Neither he nor my husband (I believe him) breathed a sound for half an hour. Of course when the plane ascended for five minutes, Floppy was released into the aisle. Oh, what a winner he was with the airhostesses. Biscuits and milk came aplenty from them. When he reached home, Bubble's ectasy was boundless. Vicky exclaimed "Eh, you fatty". The boys and the pet played for a long while.

Minto Park flats are elegant, surrounded by lawns laid with carpets of green grass. All the residents are the city's elite. Bubble and Floppy became heroes the next day. "Floppy has come by air from Delhi" declared Bubble with nose up in the air. It was a great sight to see a dozen boys and girls boisterously chanting "Floppy, Floppy". So much so that many of the residents visited us, towed by their children, to see Bubble's Floppy; as if a bride had landed. Thereafter Floppy became a piece of joy, prancing after the children of Minto Park.

The days ahead gave us joy and sorrow, but there never was a dull one. One evening we were invited at a friend's place for dinner. Floppy was left within the flat. After all, he must learn to watch the house in our absence. The next day we received brickbats from all the neighbours. Floppy's barking was loud and incessant. It seemed he wanted everyone to know of the grave injustice done to him. Chicken and ice cream for us and an empty house for him. Nothing doing, he had let us known. One of us had to stay with him whenever the family had business or party to attend to. But one Sunday we carried him with us to Tollygunge Club. I tied him to a bench outside the swimming pool and went in for a swim. Well, well! Floppy was a hit! The children, the young girls and the bearer. He got kisses, biscuits and a bone from them. Some luck, I thought. We did realise that we were in the category of seconds at Tollygunge from then on.

Floppy grew in age but vitamins injections and meat made him full of mischief and was generally chained. But whenever free, he never missed his act. We soon found plentiful single pieces of socks, tattered vests, curtains and ... The list was endless. My patience broke down and I yelled one day "Look Mangla (our maid). You are utterly careless. My velvet blouse is eaten up by cockroaches. You must have left it in the open". Mangla darted out from the kitchen and convincingly stated "No, Mem Sahib. This is Floppy and not cockroaches. Please see. He has bitten at the armpits and neckline; wherever some perspiration remained smeared".

"My God, this menace will not let us live in peace. Look you rascal" and I showed the blouse dragging Floppy along with his chain. Floppy perhaps felt his guilt. He just squatted on the floor, on all fours, mouth on the floor and eyes shut. Bubble too came out of his room, as our row was going on. He devised the punishment. Floppy to remain tied up to his bed the whole night. Floppy took this sentence stoically and gathered himself quietly underneath the bed.

Vicky came up with an idea to keep Floppy away from mischief next day. "Mummy you get this idiot a (meat) bone every day. He will chew it and thus remain occupied. You recall Masha enjoyed his bones".

I replied "Masha did not spoil any thing of ours. What a good soul, I miss him Vicky".

"Now Mummy, be fair. You never let Masha inside the house. He remained chained out in the verandah. And on top of it the chowkidar kept a vigil on him the whole night".

"Son that is the correct way to rear a pet dog. But alas we are perched here on the 8th Floor. In fact, we are unfair to this poor kid. Mangla is no help either..."

Before I could finish my sentence Mangla's protest came out loud and clear "Bai Ji how often can I run up and down eight floors for this rascal. I cannot leave him down on his own. On top of it I have to look after all the chores of your house. Do I get a minute...?"

"Enough Mangla" I had to say to stop her outburst.

From the next day onwards I decided to give a dog-bone to Floppy every day. He would jump and dance to snatch the bone from my hand as I would step in the house back from the market. Both of us enjoyed this game. He chewed and played with the bone while tied up to a chair or the bed at night. For many days, possibly a week, peace prevailed in the house. No more rags of our shirts or bed sheets. I was so delighted with myself; after all Floppy was reformed. One morning I whistled at him and caressed his soft skin lovingly. I said "How are you darling" and moved away to the kitchen to supervise preparation of the breakfast.

Bubble came out with Floppy to tie him to the dinning table. His silence and gait were not usual when the table was laid. I called out for my husband, Vicky and Bubble to have their breakfast. While waiting for them I threw a small portion of omlette to Floppy "My sweet pup is grown up and so well behaved".

"My husband was busy with his breakfast and the newspaper. Bubble came out of his room and quietly proceeded with his cereal. "Where is Vicky?" I asked.

"He is in his room".

"I know that, but why is he not coming here?"

Bubble's silence was disturbing. I walked out towards Vicky's room and threw the door open. What a scene was before my eyes. Vicky was busy switching a patch to cover the hole in the bedroll. So this is it. This miserable brute has ruined my new bedroll worth Rs. 400/-. I ran back and slapped Floppy on all sides. "You idiot! You rascal! And I had believed that you were reformed" I kept on shouting, to which my children objected in still louder voices. And Floppy was howling hoarse. The only quiet soul in the room remained my husband. Thank God, the neighbours did not walk in. Our house then witnessed nothing less than a riot!

Our collective misbehaviour did no good to Floppy. Either out of sheer defiance or because of nervoursness he would create some nuisance or another. If a carpet was torn out one day, the next day one of the shoes was cut to pieces. Spoiling our bed with his wet paws or running into milk bottles to shatter them became his nefarious and routine activities. I fumed, fretted and cursed the day I let my boys bring Floppy home. Imagine my husband on tour and I by myself on my bed when I felt Floppy's paws. He wanted to ease himself. In the middle of the night I found that there was no power and hence no light. Bubble and I started descending the steps from our eighth floor in pitch darkness. Even before we had reached the sixth floor the fellow stopped moving. I knew of the misery that lay in store for me. The stairs had to be washed and cleaned up before the residents got up for their morning walk.

My heart sank within me when I opened the door one morning. Mr. Basu, the caretaker of Minto Park, a very decent gentleman walked in. "Mrs. Bhatia, please either you put on panties to Floppy or you hand him over to someone who lives on the ground floor. You do not know the trouble I go through getting the compound cleaned up. This pet of yours is so ill trained. We will miss the Governor's Cup this year if Floppy continues to behave in this way. You know, Madam, Minto Park has won this prize for the last ten years, since I came here. Our garden is the best in Calcutta and I cannot have it spoiled".

I was mute because each word of Mr. Basu, though biting, was true. "I will do something, Mr. Basu. Please accept my apology" I replied to him.

Since that day we started looking for a suitable guardian for Floppy. It would be painful to have him advise (or warn) again. The word got round to everyone in Minto Park of our intention. Not many days later Bidhan, the young milkman, stayed back to talk to me after handing over the milk bottles to Mangla. "Bai Ji, the Durwan tells me that you want to give away Floppy" he said hesitatingly.

"Yes, Bidan. We live so high up. Poor Floppy cannot move about freely" I told him.

"Bai Ji, we have a small cottage. There is only ground floor and a lot of open space. Please give him to me" Bidhan appealed.

"Look, this little fellow is priced at Rs. 800" Mangla put in a poser.

"Oh, no" I intervened. "We do not want to sell Floppy. It is for free but its new guardian must take care of him".

"Bai Ji, I do love this pup of yours" said Bidhan.

"Of course I believe you. But who will attend to him when you are out on your rounds?"

At home my mother, brother and sister are there. They will look after Floppy".

"But it is quite costly to maintain a pet dog, Bidhan", I added, asking "Can you afford it?"

"Bai Ji, milk is no problem. And we are a non-vegetarian family. Therefore, meat and bones can be given to him. Have no doubts Madam" replied Bidhan. Bidhan's "Madam" reflected his confidence in himself to take on the new responsibility. I still persisted "Bidhan, do you realise that there will be expenses of medicines, injections and doctor's fees too?"

"I earn Rs. 5000 per month, Bai Ji. I will ensure that Floppy is healthy and happy with us" was Bidhan's reply.

Vicky came out of his room just as this conversation was going on. "Mummy it is enough. Give Floppy to Bidhan. He will keep him well. I want peace in this house" declared Vicky with finality in his voice and tone. Bubble too came along but he raised no objection. He knew that he had lost because of the dog's ill manners. Floppy went away with Bidhan.

I felt relieved and lived the next few days without tension. But our house was not the same as before. The boys came home from their schools and walked into their rooms without a word. Floppy used to bark his head off as soon as he could get a sniff of Vicky and Bubble as they would alight in the lift. My shouting to silence his howling were absolutely routine. The boys laughed and jumped with their pet. In Floppy's absence I could no longer hear "My beautiful Floppy. My black honey. Oh, my sweetie pie". Each one of us was quiet and forlorn. It was as if no more chores were left for us in the house; no running for his dinner plate, bread or milk. It seemed our lives existed for Floppy. We all looked at the vacant spot where he used to sit every time we got together at the table for breakfast or dinner but said no words. The silence around us reflected the void within us.

"Bidhan bring Floppy with you when you come this evening. The children are eager to see him".

"Alright Bai Ji. Tomorrow evening at 4 p.m. Floppy will be here for you to see. Only then will you believe that I tend him ably like you people".

Our pulses beat faster the following day at 3 p.m. or even before. Vicky and Bubble came home well before their usual time lest Bidhan should take Floppy away without waiting for them. Any sound sent Mangla scurrying to the door only to return blank eyed and cursing Bidhan. Four o'clock and then five o'clock. We were all panicky. "That milkman is not coming here any more" said Bubble with despair.

"Why do you say so?" I asked anxiously. "He is the dog's owner, the master. We do not matter", replied Bubble.

"Nonsense. Bidhan cannot claim property rights on Floppy in a matter of just two days" was Vicky's wrath.

"Floppy is a priceless gem. Bai Ji, I hope Bidhan has not sold him off to make a quick buck" said Mangla, sceptical as usual.

"Dare he sell him. We will lodge an F.I.R. with the Police", came from Vicky with authority in his voice. And Vicky then directed Bubble "You go with Mani (our driver) to Bidhan's house. Make sure that Floppy is well. There should be no hanky-panky".

The evening passed, still Bidhan did not appear. Our worry showed on our faces. None of us could eat our dinner properly. Suddenly Vicky said "Mummy I am scared. I do not have the courage to say..."

"Say what?" I was trembling by then.

"Perhaps Floppy met with an accident. Bidhan had told us that his cottage is along a major road".

At these words from Vicky I swooned without a heart beat. Oh, Lord. Is it going to be Masha again. White, serene and listless body of Masha in Vicky's arms. That horrifying scene of yesteryear rose before my eyes. I felt choked with agony and self-guilt. Why did I give Floppy away to Bidhan, my conscience questioned me. Floppy was just two years old, a kid only. He would have learnt to behave. Were Vicky and Bubble not naughty? They too were a nuisance for neighbours. Vicky and Bubble were not given away. Just because Floppy was an animal. Now I am the killer of an innocent, mute pup. I tossed in my bed with a heavy head all night long.

I walked about near the main door well before daybreak, waiting for Bidhan. He usually came at 5.30 a.m. to deliver milk to us. I could hear the lift stopping at our floor, In spite of a throbbing heart full of doubts I flung the door open.

"Why did you not come yesterday? Where is floppy. Bidhan? Is he safe?" I was panting with anger.

"Bai Ji, maaf karo (forgive me). Some guests came to our house. In fact they were considering my sister for marriage with their son. The boy is B.A. pass..."

"All right, all right, that is enough. Positively bring Floppy at 4 p.m. this evening. No more stories, please". I was still restless. Bidhan did not guage my pain and went away with disbelief at my concern for floppy whom I was so keen to banish only a week ago.

That afternoon was repeated like the one before. We were all there: Vicky, Bubble, Mangla and I. Tense, quiet and scores of unpleasant forebodings in our minds. Bidhan appeared at the door before time. We could hear Floppy's throatful barking even before opening the door. And lo, Floppy bounced out of Bidhan's hands and darted inside the house. Vicky and Bubble ran after him. Each one would draw him to his chest, hug him, kiss him by turn and then burst with hurrahs of joys. I could not believe this burst of happiness in my house. The boys had collected a heapful of cake, bread and rusks on a plate, laced with hard bones. But Floppy was licking my feet, jumping at my hands, in the manner of kissing them. I decided there and then "Floppy is not going back children".

"Three cheers for our Mummy. Three cheers for our Floppy".

Bidhan came back after his round. I told him of the change of my heart. ❑❑

One Thousand Tents

The three Mughal rulers, Akbar, Shahjehan and Aurangzeb made India a great country. In their times art, culture, architecture, administration and harmony among communities were at their best. It was an era of excellence. Alas, the successors of Aurangzeb were busy in their petty wars, each of them holding on to small parts of the great empire. The Mughal kings at Delhi were weak and dependent on the Maratha Chieftains.

The grand living of the rulers and India's all round richness attracted invaders from Central Asia. Nadir Shah of Iran was cruel and greedy. His armies looted plains of the Punjab, and cities of Delhi and Agra. India's famous peacock throne and the Koh-i-noor diamond were taken away. Left behind were widows, orphans and ruins of towns and villages.

Ahmad Shah Abdali followed Nadir Shah to conquer Northern States of India. With an army of many thousands, this Afghan adventurer overpowered the Sikh Rajas. Within months the victorius army looted the gold, jewelry and plundered harvests of zamindars from Peshawar to Lahore. But the Afghan king's eyes and mind were set on Delhi, the seat of India's rulers. His army fought many battles from Lahore to Ambala and won every one of them. But he could not conquer lands beyond Panipat where he was beaten back twice.

In 1761, Abdali came back for the third time. The fields of Panipat were once again set to determine the new ruler of India. Indian soldiers, led by Maratha Chiefs and Afghans in thousands faced each other for the do or die battle. The invader lost men and armaments in fierce fighting for a number of days.

Ahmad Shah Abdali was a worried man. The supplies of food and gun-powder were running out fast. His commanders were disheartened and wanted to go back home. One dark night, while pacing up and down furiously, the Afghan king saw a strange sight. In the enemy's camps he saw hundereds of glowing fires. He became curious and called in his advisors. After discussion, Abdali decided to send spies to investigate the mystery of fires in those tents. A few days later, the men from the intelligence branch reported,

"Your Majesty, the Indian soldiers cook their foods in scores of kitchens..." The king interjected, "Don't they run a common kitchen?"

"No, Sire".

An astonished King said, "But why? An army of men fighting together should eat together".

The man replied, "My Lord, those soldiers belong to different religions and castes. Assigned groups of men live in allotted tents and cook food on their own fires. The food, before eating, is offered to the clan's god, according to that group's religious faith. One set of persons does not touch the other group's food and clothing. They get into formations only on the battlefield".

Ahmad Shah Abdali saw a silver lining. Like lightning and idea flashed across his mind. 'He would change his strategy of fighting', thought the great tactician. The Chief of Army was asked to slow down fighting during day time. With young officers and soldiers he decided to mount a big attack after sun set. The Afghans lied low for a few days.

The Indian army was virtually lulled into a lax mood. Maratha Chiefs thought that Afghans were tired and could be laying off, like previous times, to go home. Preparations were set afoot to launch a heavy onslaught on the foreign enemy and give it a crushing defeat.

Before the fateful dawn, the Indian soldiers put up their pots to boil rice and dal, rather early in the evening. Fires were aglow in a thousand and more tents. Abdali's guerillas suddenly mounted an attack. Maratha Generals were taken by surprise. Soon the field of Panipat was littered with blood, dead bodies and broken pots and pans. Those alive ran away. Once more the battle of Panipat, in fact the battle for India, was lost to an invader.

Ahmad Shah Abdali was very intelligent and absolutely correct in bringing home a lesson for all times. "The Indian force was full of soldiers but it was not an Army. Men in a thousand tents cannot fight a common foe, because they are not united". ❑❑

The Aliens

Kalyani never misses her evening walk. A small park, surrounded by posh bungalows has seasonal blooms and neem trees. To her, amidst their solitude, come a few moments of solace after a hard day at work and before the tense evening that she apprehends at home. On that day she was dog-tired.

One evening, Kalyani on her evening round saw a crowd of 25 odd persons at corner plot. Widowed Leela Rani with her brood of an unmarried daughter and a married son with his wife and a kid lived in the house built on a part of the plot area. The commotion was due to a newly pitched tent on the other half of the plot. Kalyani pulled away Sushma, her neighbour, to give her details of the pandemonium.

"Kalyani, this is Mataji's elder son with his family. He is here to claim the unbuilt area of this plot. He says, he will build a house there".

But Sushma's long story was cut short by the man and woman who came out of the tent and made a short speech for everyone's ears.

"I am Amrik Singh, Mataji's elder son. Before my mother emigrated to Australia to stay with her daughter she had registered this part of the plot in my name. She knew I had no house of my own nor could buy a piece of land with my meagre earning".

Some one from the gathering questioned "Have you given the plot to a contractor to raise a four floor building on your part so that you can receive three floors and the basement from the builder?"

"Yes Sir, this was my plan as I have no funds for the contruction of a house" answered Amrik Singh. He continued, "Now my sisters, that one in Australia and other living in Delhi, have filed a suit against me seeking their shares in the parental property. "These wretched women are taking advantage of the Hindu Succession Act" screamed his wife. Bur Amrik Singh pushed her aside to plead with the neighbours". The laws of the land are partial to the girls of the family. How sad it is that now sisters drag their brothers to courts for their rights even after enjoying hefty dowry at the time of the wedding".

He found no takers for his reasoning and sensing this mood in the crowd he ventured further.

"Well, we are here to stay. I have signed a deal with the contractor. He will fight all people and all court cases".

These bravado sentiments amused the crowd and it dispersed. Kalyani's piece of mind was shattered. Instead of wailing around the park, she sat motionless and reflecting.

What are families coming to? Are the laws, seemingly for betterment of the society, leading to split ups of mother and son, brother and brother, brother and sister and..." she could sit there no longer moaning about the neighbour next door, or the strangers' families. Her own household was no different. All the happenings, from the day she entered into her in-laws house, rolled out before her like a Kaliedoscope.

Beautiful, convent educated, Kalyani was the youngest of four daughters of a middle level government officer. They lived in a government colony. The high middle and low were identified by the type of the quarter the official resided in. Yet the occasions to meet and mix were many; club, swimming pool or the weekly cinema shows. Kalyani was noticed and booked by the company Director's wife for her son studying in America. Mayadevi lost no time to marry Suresh on his return to Kalyani who rose to high heavens, from a 3 small room flat to a 6 room bungalow spread over 2 acres. She soon took over the responsibilities but ensured the mother-in-law retained the keys and the headship of the family. Kalyani having graduated in psychology was artful in building relationships. The two girls of Mayawati and her father-in-law too always praised Kalyani.

It was too good to last. Maheshwar Prasad, Suresh's father, collapsed of a heart attack. From the colony, they had to move to their house in Delhi, which the old man had built for his retirement days. The house was in a posh colony, but the expensive lawns and the servants attached to a government job got left behind. The life though respectable was gruelling for Kalyani. She had taken up a job, to augument Suresh's income. Two young children needed her full attention, when she returned home from work. Mayawati and her daughters who were studying for their degrees gave their helping hands. Everyday Kalyani was dog tired but the family lived peacefully and she began the next day afresh after a sound restful night.

Sunaina, the elder daughter got married and went away to Bombay with her husband. A few years later, Mini the younger one was also married, but stayed in Delhi, some 10 kilometers away from the parental home. In due course both of them raised their families. Sunaina had a boy and a girl and Mini begot a boy. Suresh made good in his company to become a General Manager. Kalyani's boys were in high school and she wondered if her service was necessary anymore. Bad luck struck again. Sunaina was widowed, she moved up to Delhi with her children. Believing it to be a temporary phase. Suresh and Kalyani raised no objection for three months. Both were shocked when Mayawati declared that Sunaina would not return to her in-laws and intended to continue in their home for good. Suresh ought to support his sister in her difficult days. Kalyani could get no peace thereafter. Day's work gave her body aches. And nights became agonising with worries of the burdens of educating and supporting one more family.

Every dawn came in with new varieties of irritating arguments. The children started quarells and the elders continued therefrom: shouting, accussing, insinuating imaginary motives. Mayawati's demands on behalf of her daughter and Sunaina's two children were unending. Suresh was reminded constantly of his duty towards his unfortunate sister; as if Kalyani's earnings could just keep pace with rising expenses and prices of food and education. Not a penny could be saved for holidaying or making another house. In fact, where was the need to build one more house, Kalyani being quite certain that Sunaina would leave their house when her son got educated and landed a job. This was not to be. Mayawati announced that she had in her WILL given away one half of the house to Sunaina. How could she bear her daughter thrown out on the street, after she closed her eyes, Mayawati told Suresh. Kalyani could visualise the dark days ahead. It was not too long before she was face to face with them. Mayawati passed away, leaving a hell behind.

Suresh, Kalyani, Sunaina have all grown grey. They are not old yet, as the children are still unmarried but fully grown up. Kalyani's boys do not talk to Sunaina's son and daughter. All of them sulk when they cannot find an unoccupied bathroom or be by themselves on the dining table. There are three bedrooms which are shared by the two families. Kalyani's boys have to settle in the drawing room for the night and their books and belongings are kept in the small store room. All the three oldies go to their jobs. Kalyani makes sure that she makes the breakfast and tiffins before Sunaina gets up. Sunaina comes home early to finish off the evening meal before Suresh and Kalyani require the kitchen. No one wants to even try to talk to the other. Eyes turn aside when any two of them accidentally become face to face. Kalyani has come to accept all this; otherwise she would have gone mad. But sometimes awake in her bed, she ruminates, "are they like a table, four legs and a top, covered at the top for the world to see them as one; yet like the four table legs, always apart!" ❑❑

Family By Proxy

The winter sun was giving its last glimpse for that day. Darkness was still transparent. Amreesh came home from his office a little later than usual. But his face showed up a somewhat funny look.

"Something new, honey?" asked Asha, his charming spouse. "Come over to the drawing room because Sonu is fast asleep. He will make hell if he is woken up and we will be burning mid-night candles", she added. Sonu is their five month old first child, a son and rather precious, by Indian tradition. Asha had laid out the tea tray and savouries to munch while they were conversing.

"It goes to my pre-marriage days..." began Amreesh.

"It is not a girl friend, I hope?" Asha mentioned just to add a bit of spicing of her own.

"You naughty little mouse", Amreesh gave her a soft pinch but continued, "It is my old, old pal, Swamy whom I have been helping for more than three years".

"You never told me before of this great friend of yours. And you have been squandering your hard earned money, at the expense of your two kids; me and Sonu", Asha became light hearted. She knew that her husband was not secretive on important matters.

"Swamy has the same grouse; raising my family at his expense. It is that chap you have seen me giving a rupee, every time I pass the Chirag Delhi over-bridge". Chirag Delhi over-bridge has traffic lights to regulate the running of vehicles. Those lights are generally red. Amreesh halts his car there and exchanges a few words with Swamy quite frequently.

"Oh, that blind man with pox marks on his face? He is in tattered rags all the time, though he keeps them clean", said Asha.

"His is a sad tale, Asha. He was born to well to do parents in a village not far from Chennai; erstwhile Madras. There were five more children in the family besides him, four girls among them. They were leading a contended life unitl their relatives, father's brothers in particular, kicked up a row. They lodged litigation over agricultural land in his father's possession. Even then his parents were persevering against all odds when a calamity visited the village. The river Kaveri washed away the entire district of Madurai".

"What bad luck! How many of the family servived?" Asha intervened with heightened anxiety.

"None except Swamy. And that too blinded in both the eyes", said Amreesh in heavy tone.

"He continued, Asha I got friendly with Swamy. I would sit with him occasionally and share jokes. One evening he asked me, Do you know God has two addresses?". When I said 'no', listen what he narrated.

'You are a goon! Swamy said laughing and continued 'God had deliberately given two addresses to his followers. He pretends he lives in temples, mosques and churches. This diverts his follower's attention from his doings. Actually God's joins the revelers in liquor bars and has lots of fun. I have no doubt the drunkards turn saintly in his Company. They shell out handsome money to beggars as they leave the bars!' Swamy burst in to laughter at his own story. His narration shook me to my ribs. That evening we had our second meal together".

Asha too gave a loud guffaw, the drink of tea choking her a little. Amreesh thumped her back to sooth the windpipe.

"Today I again sat down for a meal with him. In fact I was invited by him", Amreesh threw out a boomer.

Asha was not prepared for it. "What! He invited you?" The wife sounded cynical.

"Just listen. You can comment when I conclude. While taking the meal, Swamy took me by surprise".

He asked, 'You puzzle me Amreesh. Three year's back you used to give me ten rupees whenever you passed my way. A year later the sum was reduced to five rupees a day. And since the last five months your daily offering to me is a mere one rupee. On the one hand, the prices of all commodities are going up from day to day. On the other hand, you keep on cutting down your handouts to me. This enigma I want you to unravel for me'.

Asha, I was stunned. Never did I ponder about the reducing amounts and value of money, I was giving to him. I was bewildered because his inquiry was not only an unexpected one, it was strangely unique too. Gathering my wits I said, Swamy, the truth is that I had returned to India from England the time we met first time. I was a bachelor and my salary was pretty high compared to my colleagues, since I had British Degrees. My parents were well off and needed no support from me. Therefore I could be easy with my money which was more than my requirements anyway. Two years ago I got married, my friend. I required more money to meet the expenses of two persons. So I could spare only five rupees instead of ten. And five months ago a son was born to us. Our expenditure has escalated. I can now afford only a rupee for you.

"Can you guess, Asha, what he told me? His response was a stunning one!"

"Don't raise riddles, Amreesh. I am dying to hear his reaction", Asha refused to play the guessing game.

"Asha listen to what Swamy then said 'Amreesh your reasoning is unassailable. Now that you have cleared my doubts I must speak my mind to you. My friend, you achieved savings by cutting down on amounts rightfully due to me. Amreesh, you have been raising your family at my cost!" Totally unfair of you'.

And then he burst into a thunderous laughter. I too joined in his mirth making, at that time. "Did he seriously believe what he said?" I am confused.

Asha was not too sure of the joke. The couple always invites Swamy at Sonu's birthdays. Their Son is growing handsomely; perhaps because of Swamy's prayers and, perhaps with his money. ❑❑

Tit for Tat

Prior to independence, there was no problem in getting kids admitted into a school of their parents' choice. The Modern Model School, Lahore, enjoyed a high reputation, though it was a government school. It had large halls protected by verandas on either side. And the green and grassy ground was so huge that cricke, football, hockey and P.T. sessions were conducted simultaneously. But the panoramic school premises had one snag from the kids' point of view. The beleaguered children's cries, when punished, were inaudible to outsiders.

I was admitted to that school in Class I when I was about 6 years old. I, Deenu, Amin, David, and Surry (short for Surrinder) became close friends in a class of forty children. The four of us envied Surry who belonged to a well-to-do family. In his daily tiffin there were usually, besides chapattis and veggies, ladoos, amritees or halwa in wholesome quantities; perhaps his mother knew that he would have to share the goodies with his buddies. One day, our pal, Surry, carried a beautiful fountain pen in his pocket, a rarity for children of our age then. Little realizing that his buddies had evil eyes on his pen, he took the four of us in his car to visit his father's stationery shop. It was an eye-opener for us. The variety of diaries, writting pens, fancy table-clocks and photo frames donning pictures of fairy-like models, were awesome attractions. No wonder each of us vied to be closest to Surrinder. My heart was set on a silver plated fountain pen, a Parker, priced at Rs. 10.

A normal school day was all fun till we came to the end of the recess. Around noon we had our break time to enjoy delicacies in Surry's tiffin box. But the time thereafter seemed like hell.

Mr. Hakumat Singh, though a handsome and attractive Punjabi young man, was not very pleasant when he forced 'arithmetic' on helpess children. The afternoon sessions were literally the sessions of cries and agony. Fortunately, I happened to be the best in his sessions, especially in reciting the multiplication tables, so I generally escaped his ire.

Hakumat Singhji would introduce a new multiplication table every week. We had to sing aloud that table for more than one hour. Our sonorous voices echoed from all walls. The singing was followed by the question session. All forty of us formed a line and the teacher would ask us to answer a multiplication at random. The one who failed to answer correctly was slapped by the boy who followed him in that row and gave the correct figure. Generally, it turned out to be the weeping session because a good number failed to remember their tables. The cries were loud and proper.

Surry used to stand a place before me. He hardly ever answered correctly and I would give him a mild smack on the face. The unwritten pact was that he would get me a fountain pen after a week. And thus he was assured of light punishment till the end of the year.

However, Surrinder could not keep up his promise. I allowed him a few days grace, too, but he failed to get his father to let go of an expensive item without payment. I was livid but did not show it.

Mr. Singh's question of the day to Surrinder (how much is 12x13?) was beyond his capability. I answered 156 in a jiffy and before anybody could realize it, Surrinder's face became tomato red–the result of a resounding slap (the hardest I could manage) which I gave him. The smile of victory stretched from my one ear to the other. I looked at him sternly, conveying my resolve to give him similar treatment every day.

A wild scream went up from him. Surry cried inconsolably and many others joined him in sympathy, creating some kind of ruckus. They were stunned to see the behaviour of a 'good friend'.

The outcome was swift and sweet. I got my prize– the fountain pen. Above all, my name was etched on it! Later on, I learnt that Surrinder's mother had forced the father to relent, to save her son from a slap every day. We were on old terms again... but at a great cost to me.

The day I got my reward, I gave Surrinder a very niggardly, rather an affectionate slap. Mr. Singh called me by his chair and asked me to face the class. Unminduul of what he was hinting, I followed his instructions. Suddenly he launched an echoing full hand on my cheek. A shriek went up from me. "This is the way you ought to slap for wrong answers", he chided me.

And no one cried in sympathy with me. ❑❑

I Know, I Know, I Know

Shahpur was a bundle of sixty or seventy houses, made with mud of the soil. The peasants, shepherds, blacksmits, or carpenters were self-reliant, satisfied and peace loving. Surrounding the village was a thick forest. Thus the villagers stood both shielded and isolated from the rest of the world. The sophistication, pretentiously called civilization, never grew on them, though they were only ten kilometers from Ludhiana, the industrial hub of the Punjab. Among them lived in a pacca mansion, Shahsingh the moneylender.

Shahsingh was very fond of Parminder, his only daughter. He quarreled with his wife whenever she wanted the girl to help her in the kitchen. Her desire was to make Parminder, a proficient housewife. But the father had no worry on account of her marriage. His daughter was set to marry Surrinder, the son of Balwant Rai a friend from his school days. The marriage pact had been settled when Parminder was in her mother's womb and Surrinder was four-year-old. Strange though it may sound today, it was the practice in the Punjab fifty years back. Parminder was fifteen years old when she completed her matriculation creditably. Shahsingh was encouraged to send her to a college in Ludhiana for graduation. The father wanted his girl suitable for his son-in-law to be. Surrinder was training to be a chartered accountant. His daughter must fit into high society. Surrinder was sure to make big after gaining his professional qualification. The poor girl became a bride before learning housecraft; cooking in particular.

Surrinder and Parminder moved to Delhi after the wedding. Only two weeks later, Surrinder announced that he intended to invite Jyoti and Parkash for lunch the following Sunday. The couple decided the menu but when Surrinder wanted kheer (rice pudding) for desert, Parminder was uneasy. "I do not know how to make kheer, darling", confessed Parminder.

You can ask Malini next door. There is no need to feel shy. We will walk into their flat this evening and I will ask her to give you the recipe. There are still three days to Sunday. Surrinder made a helping offer.

"Oh, you do no such thing and expose me", Parminder protested, but added, "I will ask her diplomatically. You have no objection I hope?"

The couple settled for this arrangement. Parminder wasted no time and walked into her neighbor's house just after lunch. "I hope I am not disturbing you Malini" Parminder tried to be city-like.

"You are welcome my dear. What can I do for you?" Malini made her guest feel at ease.

"Auntie, Surrinder is keen to eat kheer. I have a rudimentary knowledge of making this pudding but I want to be sure. I need to verify from an experienced person like you if my method is correct" Parminder was extremely happy with her sophisticated approach.

"No problem. Let me first tell you the ingredients. One cup of basmati rice, the same amount of sugar plus one kilogram of milk. For seasoning you can have almonds, kaju and krishmish in reasonable quantities. Do not forget to chop the almonds and kaju. If you like pista and ilaichi you can have them also", Malini made an elaborate list.

"Auntie, I know all this. Please tell me only the method of making the dish", Parminder interrupted her mentor.

Malini ignored the immature remark and proceeded, "Take a good size pan and put the milk to boil but on low fire. I forgot to tell you to soak the rice in water a few hours earlier..."

"This is quite known to me", Parminder unceremoniously cut her short. Malini got rattled a bit but she maintained her composure.

"O.K. So far so good. As the milk gets to a boil place the soaked rice in the pan and let them stay on slow boil until the milk thickens to half its earlier volume. This is the time to put the almonds, kaju, krishmish into the milk and..."

"I knew this part all along, auntie, I wish I had told you this before hand and saved, your and my time. I am sorry, I should get along now", saying which Parminder got up to leave.

By now Malini was outraged. She decided to give the brat a lesson of her life. "Wait a minute. I should tell you the last secret. You ought to obtain a fistful of grey coal-ash from the Halwai and sprinkle it on the rice pudding. The dish will take a silver look and a magnificent taste. That will do darling", and Malini saw her neighbor to the door.

Parminder on her part felt very clever. She had got the recipe without exposing her ignorance. The kheer was duly prepared with rice, milk, condiments and coal-ash et-all. The meal and the desert were served as soon as Surrinder came from his office. Parminder had an air of pride on her face expecting compliments from a gratified husband.

"What have you done? Why this coal-ash? Whoever made you make this rot?" Surrinder threw out the mouthful into the washbasin.

Parminder got scared. She named Malini from whom she had got the recipe. She swore that she followed her advice to the last word. This is outrageous, thought Surrinder and he immediately walked into his neighbors flat. Ofcourse he held his calm and respectfully asked the lady for the details of the queer episode.

Malini expected Surrinder. "Calm down my son. Take the kheer that I have prepared for you. Your wife made me mad with her I Know, I Know, I Know refrain to whatever I told her this morning. Beta ignorance is no curse. To pretend otherwise is arrogance, which can be ruinous. All of us need to learn a lot during our lifetime. Those who want to learn something new must be modest and patient. I had no intention of hurting you or her", Malini ended on a grave note.

Surrinder and Parminder remembered Malini's words for all times to come. Parminder learnt many new things besides cooking. ❑❑

My Grandmother Number Four

It was an unusual day in 1955 when I travelled from Manchester, in England, to Charleroi near Brussels, in Belgium. Though summer time, it was raining throughout the journeys–in trains and in a ferry across the English Channel. I reached my destination but by the time I managed to meet the Training Officer, Frank Anatolia of A.C.E.C. (manufacturer of Heavy Electrical Equipment), the clouds had gathered for a downpour. Frank had not arranged any accommodation for me for which he felt very guilty. He decided to request his aunt, Lilleette Bordeaux, who owned a three-bedroom house to put me up. At this late hour she was our only hope.

Lilleettee Bordeaux was a short, frail woman hardly five feet in height. She was eighty years old as Frank informed me on the way to her house. A bag of bones, she was sheathed in muslin-thin long skirt, high-neck blouse and a scarf tied on her head. The wrinkles on her face, one on either cheek, added grace to her otherwise unblemished skin. But her sparkling eyes, somewhat invasive, left me gaping at her. So old yet so alive!

Madame was neither pleased nor unhappy to see us. She did not even ask us in. Frank then told her that he had brought me over so that I could take shelter, from the rain.

"I don't keep lodgers", she said. "They need so many facilities. I cannot cook".

I didn't know French but sensed Frank's predicament. "I will manage everything myself and I shall eat elsewhere", I was desperate.

Madame looked uncomfortable but finally relented and asked us in. A room with a wide bed, a cupboard, a table and a chair was shown to me. On another table was a white ceramic washbowl and a jug which was later filled with water for the night time necessities. It is then I learned that in Belgium there are no in-house bathrooms, only community swimming and bathing houses.

"How much will he pay me?" she asked and then answered herself, "I will charge 85 francs per day".

My stipend was 110 francs a day. I wondered how I would arrange my three meals and all the other expenses from the remaining 25 francs. Frank looked at me. There was no room to negotiate and I agreed to her terms. I felt so secure when I rested in that soft bed and spent a dreamless night.

The morning was difficult. I had to make do with a jug of water and the washbowl on the table; I brushed, shaved and bathed using very little water. I was worried that I should not drop water on the carpet. And then I carried the soiled water to the toilet and washed it clean. I also made the bed and dusted the room. This became my daily routine. There was no choice!

"*Bonjour, Madame*", I said with an effort to please the old lady. My Punjabi-French could tickle only a smile out of her.

"*Merci*, thank you!" she responded but the flicker of smile soon vanished. Then she walked into the room and said, "Take bus no. 82 to your workplace".

I felt happy that she was satisfied with my efforts at cleanliness. And she went away without even looking at me.

I used to finish all my outside chores including meals for the day before returning to my abode. One evening, as I returned, I saw the light in the house was bright and she too was dressed up. I could then visualize her in her younger days. Her transparent skin when full of flesh must have been creamy white. (She told me later that she was as white as lily when she was born hence her name Lilleette). I imagined her cheeks must have been rose-pink and her eyes must have had the same arrogance that was being reflected now. She must had many suitors in her younger days. I had picked up a few words of French during the day from one of the workers. So I came out of my room after depositing my briefcase, and took courage to say, "Madame, beaux yeux, very beautiful when young".

The mixture of French, English and Punjabi accent brought a hearty laughter from her.

"*C'est bien*, that's good?" she proffered.

I was surprised but muttered "*Merci*".

"I know little English, you know little French. We can teach each other and have fun", was her unexpected but gracious offer.

I no longer felt tense. By the time the evening wore out, I had told her about my family and my favourite foods and likings. She in turn told me of her marriage to an army captain who rose to be a colonel. They had a son, their only child. Her husband wanted to see her beautiful always. More children would have spoiled her figure and she smiled while saying it. For once I saw her relaxed.

As I prepared to go to my room she said, "I take a sandwich and coffee for supper. You too should do likewise. Wait here I will bring supper for you". Without waiting for my response she disappeared. More than my stomach, it was my heart which relished that supper.

"Madame supper *tres bien* very good. *Merci*, thank you" I blurted out.

I could hear her laugh even after I had gone inside my room. From that evening onwards we became friends.

The days that followed were marvellous. I was getting breakfast besides supper. She would even make me a late night coffee.

On my asking for more details of her married life she told me that the first tragedy that struck the family was when her son was killed in the First World War. The colonel, her husband, was inconsolable. He too had died a year later. His son's wife remarried but left behind the grandson who was six years old. Madame enjoyed bringing up that boy who also joined the Belgian Army. Then Hitler unleashed the terrible Second World War and the young boy was killed at the border. Madame burst out crying remembering her grandson. She brought out his photograph. He looked extremely handsome. Anyone would cry on such a tragic tale and so did I. Suddenly I drew her to myself, wiped her tears, and patted her skinny cheeks.

I went to the kitchen that evening and made the supper for both of us. Neither had any words to say!

The remaining twelve days passed off whith unimaginable comfort. We exchanged pleasing anecdotes for long hours till late into the night.

On the weekend she invited Frank and his family for a trip to Brussels. We had a gala time at the Russian Circus show, and lunch at an Italian restaurant besides visiting the Waterloo war fields where Napoleon was checkmated. Among all of us the old lady seemed to be having the best time. She looked so young, so beautiful! I too remember that weekend to this day. In the joyful days I inwardly feared the day of my departure. It arrived too soon. Frank came over to help me settle my account. I had worked out that thirteen days lodging charges amounted to 1105 francs. In addition, there would be extras for my washing at least, even if she didn't charge me for the breakfast and suppers. Therefore, I had changed my travellers cheques to have 1500 francs on me.

"How much does Sam owe you?" Frank asked.

"Nothing".

Both of us were aghast! "Sam reminded me of my grandson", she continued, "The days I spent with him were full of life. I am living once again. God bless you, my son!" She held me in her arms and kissed me with utmost affection.

Tears came rushing to my eyes and in the Indian tradition I touched her feet.

Frank explained to her that in the Indian tradition that was the manner in which a grandson said farewell to his granny. I had three grandmothers till I met Madame Lilleette Bordeaux who became my grandmother number four. I always sent her Christmas gifts till she lived. I terribly miss the box of chocolates she used to send me every Christmas! ❑❑

Teacher, Sir

India's Independence divided the country into two parts. I happened to be at Lahore on that fateful day. Chaos and mayhem in the city was traumatic. A few months of my schooling were lost by the time I reached Pune from Lahore. My father, an officer in the Air Force, was posted there. We were housed in a spacious bungalow whose cool and green ambience wore off the stress and trauma of ghastly days. But my admission into Class I in a convent school gave me discomfort for many months. To begin with I was withdrawn, shy and frightened in my class. On one pretext or another, I was awarded punishment, of a few cane-lashes.

But Lajo, Mainka, Pinki, Dev, Arjun and Nitin, my classmates, were great comforters. Our group would wander off during the recess period, to remote corners of the school compound. There were many varieties of flowering bushes, and we stayed secure under their fragrance for that half hour. Near the boundary wall, grew many kind of trees. My friends introduced me to the 'imli' (tamarind) tree the sour-sweet taste of which was heavenly (I get the blissful feeling even today). There was also a tree of red 'Ratees' (beads). At the end of the day, we stealthily plucked the beads to make necklaces. We did not dare to wear them during school hours for fear of severe punishment. It was, however, good fun playing 'gypsies' wearing those colourful necklaces on the way home.

The teacher of 'History and P.T.' (He and the priest were the only male tutors, the others were nuns) was paunchy and bald. He spoke in a peculiar accent which made us giggle, never outwardly though. He carried a rod of solid wood which was well polished. It was commonly employed during the P.T. sessions to straighten our arms and legs. The P.T. drill and exercises were followed by the 'Recess Period', our happiest hour in the daily routine. Sauntering around and gobbling our food, we copied our teachers. Each of us played a part. Mainka acted as Sister Maria. Bulging eyes and red faced, she would admonish the rest of us because none of us could spell 'vicereine' correctly. Dev played Father Hugh superbly, waxing his cane, eager to give a lash or two to anyone who faltered or recited incorrectly the multiplication table of the day.

I was excellent at 'rhyming' and mimicking the History teacher. The group took to singing the rhymes made by me.

One day, Sister De Silva overheard us while we were having our rhyming session during the break. Her puckered ears and red-shot eyes stared at us.

Dev said, "Sister D (devil) is going to tell all to the P.T. teacher".

"She will add salt and pepper too", was Arjun's fear. We knew that her oft repeated words, "Spare the rod and spoil the child" would wreak havoc soon.

Scared, we returned post-haste to the class, quickly gobbled the contents of our tiffins and were getting ready to face the onslaught when the History teacher walked in. He growled and looked stern. His polished 'ruler' sat shining on the table. He began, "Today I shall do poetry instead of history. How about a few couplets from you, Preeti darling? I learn you have become a great poet".

I was trembling with fear and stood there silent and still.

After a few moments of silence, he said, "Come on, Fellows, any one of you?" Getting no response he looked at me, "Ah, Preeti, let us hear a few couplets from you". There was a sneer in his voice.

I was too stiff to even breathe. None of the others spoke. There was the silence of stones in our classroom. All heads were bowed down.

His voice boomed. "How should I treat you for making fun of teachers?"

There was no response from our side. Those moments, still and soundless, were agonizing. And then a surprise hit us. His stern looks turned benign. He said in a slow tone, "I am not punishing anyone. Listen to me, instead of parodying with foolish stuff, use your telent constructively. I trust you will be careful in future".

There were audible sighs of relief. I stood there like a log all the while. "I am very sorry, Sir", I could barely whisper the words. Yet, I sincerely meant what I had said.

I followed the teacher's advice. I and my other friends, besides looking after our households and children, are now good dancers, painters and radio and T.V. artists too. And I often wonder how many times the saying, 'Spare the rod and spoil the child' has wrought havoc on the minds of growing children! ❑❑

Bridging the Gap

"How come you know so many nice things, Daadi", said six-year-old Anushka. She with her brother Mayank and mother had arrived from Dubai in the morning. They were all at the dining table preparing to go to bed early that evening.

"What nice things, darling?" asked the grandmother.

"The songs, the poems, and those stories of kings", Anushka elaborated. She added, "I am bored at the school, Daadi, only counting from 1 to 100, and on and on. No one tells us stories like you, Daadi".

Daadi drew Anushka to her lap, cuddled her and kissed her. "I will tell you a new story tomorrow. You must sleep well tonight". The youngest and the oldest made a pact.

Twenty-four hours sped by; the grandparents busy in their daily chores and the children with their mother visiting the relatives. All of them got together again at dinner time.

"Daadi, remember?" Anushka winked at her grandmother.

"I do. Daadi is to tell us a story", Mayank chipped in happily.

"Listen carefully to the story. I will ask a question at the end. Ten marks for the best answer". With this preface Daadi continued.

"A few hundred years ago there were no schools like the ones you have today. Gurukuls were the only places of learning. Anand Ashram, on the banks of the River Ganga on a mountainous slope had gained high reputation. Situated a few kilometres away from a village, six or seven hamlets were spread over an acre or two. The ashram was engulfed by rows of pine trees on all sides. A *pugdandi* (unpaved irregular path) connected it to the village. The route led through a waterfall more than 100 m deep. The ashramites swam through the running waters going to and coming back from the village but this was required only occasionally.

Maharishi Giananand agreed to educate the three sons of Maharaj Bal Bahadur, the king of Uttarkashi. The boys along with other students were tutored in yoga, tending the cattle, meditation, besides statecraft and martial arts. Their life was not easy but the princes had been forewarned of the hardships they would face. They spent a year usefully and happily. They had worked hard and cleared all the tests given to them from time to time. Hence they eagerly waited for the annual vacation. Their preparations to go home were on.

Kanwar Bhadur, the eldest, used to go to the village daily before and after his duties at the ashram. He got tailored robes for his parents and himself, besides buying locally made artefacts. The prince wanted his parents to appreciate that he had remembered them always. The offerings were a token of gratitude and affection towards them. Moreover, his grasp of the statecraft was excellent.

Suryaprakash Bhadur, the midde prince, was brave, daring and ambitious. But he was secretive too, quite opposite to his name. No one could ever find out what he was up to. He usually disappeared when the others at the ashram selpt. Somewhere deep in the forest, he would practice horse-riding, archery and wrestling with some folks from the village. Surya wanted to impress his father with his warrior-like abilities. He definitely wanted to be the commander-in-chief of the king's army when his brother took over the reins. He had his eyes on the adjoining territories of Chamba and Garhwal and was determined to annex them sooner than later. The ashram was the training ground for those adventures.

The youngest, Kiran Bahadur, was studious and unassuming. Very few of his ashram mates knew of his royal origin. Always available for others, he promptly attended to their problems, be they personal or otherwise. He was a meticulous organizer, too. He arranged in the ashram special functions on all festivals. In his spare time he would collect teams of six or seven boys to plant flower-beds, clean up hamlets or go into the forest to cut logs as also to collect firewood for the kitchen. He continued to follow his routine though the annual vacation was so near.

Two days before the holidays a message came that the king's men were waiting in the village to fetch the princes back home. The rest of the pupils were also busy packing. And then the winds from the east started blowing fast and furious. With the storm, dark black clouds gathered over the mountains. Lightning flashed frequently, dazzling in the darkness. The clouds thundered like two armies booming their guns at their opponents. The rain poured incessantly in streams. The waterfall swelled with roaring torrents. The ashram was cut off from the world outside.

Kanwar was very upset and stayed in bed waiting for the rains to stop. He was not going to wet his feet.

Surya was furious, too, and threw his fists skyward, threatening the rain gods.

But soon Kiran and his team appeared carrying on their shoulders a log of wood. They cared little for their drenched bodies and toiled till the log was placed across the waterfall. The second team then took over and then the third. Thus they placed two more logs alongside the first one, making a stable bridge over the ferocious waters. The rains did not stop but the pupils crossed over to go to their homes for the holidays.

Thereafter the ashram was never isolated from the village.

"Now, tell me children, whom do you consider the best of the three princes and why?" asked Daadi.

Mayank answered first, "Kiran obviously is the best because he is a team man".

"Daadi I also like him. He was so caring and loving of others", said Anushka.

"Both of you get 10 marks each. And do you know what the Guru did? He ordered Kanwar and Surya to stay back and work in the ashram during the holidays".

"Serves them right. They were so selfish, Daadi", said Anushka.

The evening turned out to be a pleasand one. ❑❑

www.ingramcontent.com/pod-product-compliance
Lightning Source LLC
LaVergne TN
LVHW050551160826
845677LV00011B/2276

* 9 7 9 8 6 6 2 7 9 0 9 7 1 *